ABOUT THE AUTHORS

Andrew Green (1927-2004) began hunting ghosts in war-time London in 1944 and over the next 60 years investigated many hundreds of reports of ghosts in castles, stately homes and private houses throughout Great Britain. From the 1970s until his death, he actively promoted the scientific investigation of ghosts, helping develop many of the techniques routinely used by serious ghost hunters today. A respected lecturer and authority, he published 17 books including *Our Haunted Kingdom* (1973), *Phantom Ladies* (1976), *Ghosts of Today* (1980), *Haunted Kent Today* (1999) and the posthumously published *Unknown Ghosts of the South-East* (2005). He saw at least two ghosts for himself.

Alan Murdie is a lawyer and psychical researcher. He has investigated numerous cases of ghosts and hauntings in Britain and abroad. He is chairman of the Ghost Club (founded 1862) and chairs the Spontaneous Cases Committee of the Society for Psychical Research. He has written and broadcast extensively and writes monthly columns on ghosts and hauntings for *Fortean Times* magazine and the website europaranormal.com. He has seen one apparition and witnessed poltergeist phenomena.

Ghost Hunting: A Practical Guide

The New Edition

By

Andrew Green and edited by Alan Murdie

Published 2016 by arima publishing

www.arimapublishing.co.uk

ISBN 978 1 84549 687 6

Printed and bound in the United Kingdom

arima publishing
ASK House, Northgate Avenue
Bury St Edmunds, Suffolk IP32 6BB
t: (+44) 01284 700321

www.arimapublishing.com

Cover Image: An upper window of a haunted property in Ealing, London, taken in September 1944 by Andrew Green which has been interpreted as possibly showing the apparition of a 12 year-old girl.

INTRODUCTION TO THE NEW EDITION

by Alan Murdie

This book *Ghost Hunting: A Practical Guide* by Andrew Green (1927-2004) is one which every ghost hunter should read.

Not only was it the first ever book of its kind aimed at introducing ghost hunting as a scientific activity to the wider public, but it also remains one of the best of its type yet written for the beginner, a work of lasting influence that will assist many would-be ghost hunters today. For a book which saw its first edition in 1973 it still stands up exceptionally well, providing a comprehensive introduction for the complete new-comer to the field, as well as setting down valuable advice and guidance for those who have already embarked upon investigating haunted homes and places for themselves. At the time of first publication, Andrew Green had already acquired nearly 30 years of practical experience in ghost hunting from a scientific perspective, having begun his investigations in 1944. It is a book which places the topic within the disciplines of psychical research and parapsychology, seeking to incorporate what has been established in these fields as a foundation for investigating and understanding what are popularly called ghosts. As a result, it remains an ideal book for beginners seeking to take a rational approach to this most challenging of areas in psychical research.

As well as providing practical advice and guidance, *Ghost Hunting: A Practical Guide* has three important messages if you want to get seriously involved with investigating reports of ghosts and hauntings today.

Firstly, it is a book which encourages would-be investigators to lay aside preconceptions, particularly the idea that ghosts are the spirits of the dead. If we already knew this as a certainty, what would be the point of investigating? Andrew Green did not endorse carrying out ghost hunts on the basis that investigators were seeking spirits, for this was already to prejudge the issues. The subject of ghosts and hauntings is a controversial one about which both sceptics and believers can become very emotionally involved – notwithstanding the fact that one side in the argument asserts such things do not exist! Ideally, personal beliefs on spirits should not come into work in this area, rather the approach should be to gather and examine evidence, regardless of where it may lead.

Principally, we cannot be sure – at least to a scientific standard of proof - that spirits actually exist. What we can be certain about is that many people experience apparitions and report strange phenomena that cannot be readily explained. Some places seem particularly prone to generating these sort of experiences and they are called "haunted" as a result. However, at most, the idea that these experiences are caused by the spirits of the dead is just one of a number of possible explanations to be tested. This has important implications for conducting research.

Secondly, as you will find, it is a book which emphasises that ghost hunting requires far more than simply turning up at a reputedly haunted house and waiting to see if a ghost appears.

In particular, it emphasises the importance about gathering facts and information about the location at which the ghost is reported and obtaining details from the witnesses. The idea that ghost hunting is all about trying to catch ghosts on camera or recording them on other instruments is a mistake that many beginning ghost hunting in the 21st century make in their enthusiasm. It should be remembered that without witness reports at the outset there would be no cases of hauntings to investigate. If we are to learn more about ghost experiences, it is necessary to collect evidence from people who have actually seen or experienced apparitions and haunting phenomena. This book provides a valuable introduction to collecting testimony from witnesses and some of the pitfalls. It is also necessary for researchers to thoroughly understand the physical aspects of the location where a ghost is reported. Without such understanding researchers may be prone to making the same errors as witnesses can do, misperceiving natural events. Haunting manifestations can often turn out to have an entirely normal explanation. Accordingly, this book concentrates upon examining the physical aspects of the locality to rule out natural causes for events which may be mistaken as signs of ghostly activity.

As regards equipment to be taken on investigations, it should be remembered that the role of equipment is not to detect ghosts (there are currently no 'ghost detecting' devices in existence) but to attempt to record tangible and measurable evidence by way of instrumentation that may provide some corroboration as to what the witnesses have already reported, or provide some insight on the nature of the experience, for example to see if a natural cause may be identified. Whilst a photograph taken at a reportedly haunted location might suggest that something strange or anomalous is happening, it should not be taken as definitive proof in itself, but often simply the stimulus for further study and investigation. Many items of equipment deployed by today's ghost hunters have an unproven value to paranormal study – the case for the negative ion detector (NID) and electromagnetic field (EMF) meters being useful and scientific tools has not been demonstrated beyond pure conjecture and supposition. With every piece of equipment, it is of crucial importance that one knows how to operate it, and also understand both the capabilities and the limitations of the device or instrument concerned and sources of error. This is particularly true with cameras of all varieties. The photographic evidence for ghosts is nowhere near as strong as was once considered, and investigators need to be aware of how digital cameras and camera phones can generate peculiar images which are wrongly labelled as ghosts.

Other more basic items, such as the thermometer, remain important. They are used to objectively measure extreme and inexplicable ambient temperature changes both in haunted locations and in the séance room.

Thirdly, and perhaps the most important aspect of ghost hunting as a serious activity which Andrew Green emphasised, is that common sense and rational thinking must be applied to the whole subject. One of his key pieces of advice is "The true investigator should question everything" – and this includes the claims and assumptions of psychic researchers and particularly what is today popularly represented - or rather misrepresented - as ghost hunting in the media. In the last 20 years, ghost hunting as an activity has increased in popularity in the UK and USA, with marked leanings towards spiritualist beliefs. Increasing numbers of people on both sides of the Atlantic engage in ghost hunting as a hobby, encouraged by popular television shows. Justly treated with scepticism and frequently ridicule by much of the viewing public and most critics, such TV programmes often regularly involve the use of self-proclaimed psychics and mediums, few of whom have been subject to any independent scrutiny or testing. Despite ever sophisticated gadgetry being used, many investigations end up attempting to communicate with 'the dead' rather than discovering the mechanics of the phenomena, or whether there is really anything paranormal happening at all. How readings from instruments might fit in with any particular theory about haunting experiences provides a major challenge in itself and there are many difficult areas and almost no certainties. The fact that a person claims to be a psychic does not mean s/he is one; equally the possibility that a person does have extrasensory powers should not be dismissed. On a more mundane level, claims made about the history of a site should not be automatically accepted without going back to original sources of any claim wherever possible.

Andrew Green emphasised checks, verification and corroboration and obtaining independent opinions throughout an investigation at all stages, even if these challenge one's own personal beliefs, and as befits the goal of obtaining credible and scientific data. Alternative explanations must be considered. In a field where there few certainties and so many contradictory and competing beliefs, taking a rational approach is the soundest and most essential advice of all.

Who was Andrew Green and what were his own views about ghosts and ghostly phenomena?

Born in Ealing in London in 1927, Andrew Green's interest in the paranormal was sparked when his father took him to a now-demolished property at Montpelier Road, Ealing in London in September 1944. The house had stood abandoned for ten years, and enjoyed a grim local reputation for suicides and murder and was widely believed haunted. After a disturbing personal experience in which he felt unseen hands touching him, Andrew Green took an external photograph of the empty building which, when developed, seemed to suggest the figure of a girl at a window (local stories subsequently blamed a ghostly girl for causing suicides at the house). In later years he met many people who had experienced strange noises, smells or observed unusual animal reactions inside the property, by then divided into flats, although many other stories and claims about its history were never corroborated. The property was finally demolished in 1971.

Later taking a Bachelor degree in science and a Masters in philosophy at the London School of Economics, Andrew Green continued his psychical investigations through the 1950s and 1960s, whilst pursuing a number of careers and business interests. After experience in publishing in the 1960s he turned to writing and broadcasting, beginning research in the early 1970s for his extensive gazetteer *Our Haunted Kingdom* (1973) covering over 300 contemporary hauntings in Great Britain and Ireland. The book marked a return to the survey based approach to hauntings and apparitions which had characterized the early Society for Psychical Research which he joined in 1972. He went on to produce a further volume covering specifically female apparitions nationwide with *Phantom Ladies* (1976) and a further 400 cases of all classes of haunting phenomena were listed in *Ghosts of Today* (1980).

These contemporary studies confirmed that healthy, sober people experienced a range of ghostly phenomena, with visual experiences being the most common. Sounds were also reported, including voices, footsteps and music, and more occasionally sensations of being touched or of strange smells. The feelings of a presence and feelings of cold and strange animal reactions also featured. Andrew Green believed that these experiences were far more common than was generally realised but only a fraction were being recorded and properly studied by researchers. He produced further local and regional books on hauntings such as *Ghosts of The South East* (1977) *Haunted Sussex Today* (1994) and *Haunted Kent Today* (1997) with his last being his posthumously published *Unknown Ghosts of the South East* (2005).

As well as being fascinated by contemporary reports and experiences, Andrew Green was most keen to promote their scientific exploration and investigation more widely amongst the public, hoping to counteract the fear and superstition which such ghostly phenomena so often engender. From the end of the 19th century, psychical researchers had often taken equipment into séance rooms to attempt to record spirit manifestations and in the 20th century this approach began to be adopted with investigating haunted houses. From the 1960s serious researchers routinely took equipment such as tape recorders, video cameras and thermometers on investigations into haunted premises. It soon became a truism that most alleged hauntings are attributable to natural causes, particularly noises (e.g. problems with plumbing, birds in the roof or structural faults) and equipment may be able to eliminate these. If written today, more attention might also be devoted to the cultural and social settings in which ghost experiences occur and shape perceptions, but for practical investigation work a good grounding in the physical basics of a location is an essential prerequisite.

Other ghostly experiences have psychological causes within the mind of the witness who may be subject to irrational fears or beliefs. Andrew Green shared the opinion of Tom Perrott (1921-2013), a long-serving chairman of the Ghost Club who remarked, "In many cases my ghost hunting equipment consists of a note pad, a pencil and a sympathetic ear." However, a number of cases defied ready explanation, though with the exception of some well observed poltergeist incidents such as the Rosenheim case in Germany in 1967 and the Enfield poltergeist of 1977-79, relatively little hard evidence has been obtained.

Andrew Green met his second wife, Norah Cawthorne through one of his local investigations in 1976 and they settled at Mountfield, near Robertsbridge in Sussex from where he continued to work and write for the rest of his life. As well as writing books, from the 1970s and up until his death in 2004, he sought to promote interest and understanding in the scientific aspects of the paranormal with articles in a wide range of publications and lectures to different organisations. He was pleased to see parapsychology become a recognised discipline and course taught at a number of universities in Great Britain.

Variously described as "Britain's Spectre Inspector", "our leading Ghost Buster" and "a secular exorcist" in the press and media, for five years he worked as a consultant to two local authorities in the south of England. He contributed articles on ghostly experiences and parapsychology to professional journals and publications covering medicine and health, social work, education and law enforcement, providing guidance to practitioners on how to handle individuals, families or patients who might report ghostly experiences. He also broadcast extensively, and from 1971 he established a long-running series of adult education courses at further education colleges across Kent and Sussex. Andrew Green was a founding member of the Association for the Scientific Study of Anomalous Phenomena (ASSAP) and Honorary President of the East Anglian-based Borderline Science Investigation Group. He was also the inspiration for the fictional ghost investigator 'Chris Bishop' in the novel *The Dark* (1980) by James Herbert and he was portrayed by Terrence Hardiman in 'Andrew Green - the Ghostbuster' an edition of the ITV series *'Strange But True?'* in 1997 recalling his investigations at the Royal Albert Hall, the Seven Stars Inn at Robertsbridge and the haunted Dreamland fairground attraction at Margate.

As regards his own perspectives, Andrew Green in many ways was a convinced materialist and drew firm boundaries between scientific theories and any other sort, particularly seeking to exclude anything which smacked of a spiritual or mystical approach when investigating a case. This is reflected in *Ghost Hunting: A Practical Guide.*

There is no doubt people experience apparitions, in states of normal consciousness, though a considerable percentage often occur in a state of relaxation or linked with sleep, or when "not thinking about anything in particular". Green had a number of personal experiences like this himself over the years, and he was fully convinced he had witnessed at least one, and possibly two, full apparitions in his lifetime. The first was a black terrier dog seen at the home of an uncle at Sidmouth in 1952 which had been the pet of the previous owners, and the second was the apparition of a teenage boy at a hotel run by friends in the South East of England in the late 1960s. On several other occasions he had also witnessed shadowy figures at different locations.

Andrew Green took the view that most examples of what are classed as hauntings could be explained by telepathy or psychokinesis produced by the living. Around 40% of ghosts in his estimation were being generated by living people rather than representing psychic traces of the dead. He believed that during times of stress, such as physical pain or emotional upset, the brain projects a telepathic image beyond it. A subject standing on the site to which the image is being transmitted would, if a telepathic recipient, probably see the image. He considered the telepathically created picture, or telepathic hallucination, can exist for months, or even years in the locality, and will therefore "outlive" the agent. He thought there was an electromagnetic basis to these mental images, later perceived as hauntings, being produced at the moment of death by the person whose apparition was subsequently seen or by a living person who was emotionally connected with the place or the individual concerned. He believed that such mental images were persistent, capable of continuing after the death of the person who originally created them.

An argument against all visual apparitions being pure telepathy is that the form may be witnessed on different occasions, suggesting that the apparitional form has some independent existence. As Dr Alan Gauld pointed out in his book *Mediumship and Survival: A Century of Investigation* (1983), the ESP which must be occurring in a multi-witnessed case far exceeds anything normally recorded in laboratories and points to the apparition having some degree of spatial reality, which is external to mind of the observer. Thus, in one sense, ghosts might be understood as spatially fixed psychic effects that persist after death. But on what level of reality? This has proved very much a question for philosophers and scientists in the past and remains a challenge for those willing to go beyond the boundaries of materialist notions and ideology today.

Similarly, with poltergeist activity Andrew Green thought that psychokinesis on the part of the living would provide an explanation in the majority of cases; he had first-hand experience of poltergeist activity surrounding a 15 year-old girl at Battersea, London in 1956. Much of the scientific evidence for psychokinesis has been achieved in laboratory trials with moving targets such as falling dice or influencing random number generators; there has been relatively little research with trying to move or influence objects outside controlled conditions. One of the founders of the Society for Psychical Research Frederic Myers maintained that there was a clear separation between cases of object movements and apparitions, but since the 1970s the realisation has grown that the distinctions drawn by psychical researchers may not be as clear-cut as previously thought. Poltergeist phenomena can occur in the context of place-centred hauntings, with no obvious living focus and despite changes in occupiers. A good example is the Seven Stars pub in Robertsbridge, Sussex, close to his home which Green himself went on to investigate over a thirty-two year period between 1971-2003, notwithstanding twelve changes in licensees and their families. Similarly, a study of press reports of ghosts and haunting in the UK undertaken by myself for the first half of 2007 suggested that some 52% of cases involving object movements also mentioned an apparition or a visual experience of some kind.

At present, no current theory adequately explains all ghostly experiences, although most reported cases will have something to offer for the open-minded investigator, whatever their causation. Work in this field will help shed light on these questions given that existing models of the brain, the mind and psi experiences are all incomplete.

My personal connection with Andrew Green goes back many years. I first read Andrew Green's books from the mid-1970s and began corresponding with him in 1986. A decade late in the mid-1990s I got to know him and his wife Norah very well, and I began to share in teaching on the adult education courses covering ghosts and psychical research run by him which he had pioneered in 1971. Over the years I shared many discussions with him, and he answered numerous enquiries that I and others made calling on his experience. I also have had many opportunities to apply the practical guidance and advice he gave on my own ghost investigations over the years and have invariably found it sound. Following Andrew Green's death in 2004 I became literary executor to the Green estate on behalf of his widow Norah until her death, and now act on behalf of his step-son Paul Cawthorne, who has generously granted me access and custody of Andrew Green's extensive archive and records.

With this new edition, of *Ghost Hunting: A Practical Guide* I have made a number of changes to the text with the permission of the Green estate. Throughout I have sought to preserve the original text save for a small amount of material which has been removed from the book where it has been superseded. In this edition I have also included some footnotes for more specialist readers and those revisiting this book after many years (the publishing fashion having been against them at the time of original publication). Some of the references may seem advanced for an introductory book such as this, but any serious student who may have his or her interest fired by this work and the search for truth will, sooner or later, wish to move on to consider the more advanced literature in this vast area. I have removed a list of organisations concerned with psychical research included in the 1973 edition as many of them proved regrettably defunct but an updated book list is included adding a number of titles drawn from Andrew's own library or published since his death.

Some new information on parapsychology has been added and in inserting material into this book, I have drawn upon subsequent writings and lectures which Andrew delivered and information on areas he thought worthy of experiment and exploration, as well as having gained further insights into his extensive research from his archive (like many researchers there were many reports and cases he never wrote up or published).

I feel confident that Andrew Green would have approved of the majority of changes, since I have included the fruits of many discussions with him, about how he viewed his own work with the passage of time and revisions he would like to have seen made, particularly with reference to the so-called 'orb' phenomenon. He always considered it was important for ghost hunters to keep up with the latest developments in parapsychology and psychical research, in keeping with his scientific perspective, and was personally always prepared to update, revise and extend his views in light of latest findings and new information that emerges. I am pleased to include an Appendix condensed from a chapter of the book *Ghostology* (2016) by Steve Parsons, another psychical researcher and field investigator who was originally inspired by this work as a further enhancement of the text.

Whilst Andrew Green did not know the answers – and we clearly still do not - he certainly believed in looking for them in a rational way. This new edition of his classic work hopes to continue and build upon the basic case he set down for doing so and also provide a practical memorial to a dedicated researcher, original thinker and valued friend in this most fascinating and challenging of subjects.

Acknowledgements: A number of people have provided great help and encouragement with this new edition of Andrew Green's *Ghost Hunting: A Practical Guide*. Principally these include Andrew's widow the late Norah Green and her son Paul Cawthorne who both supported the idea of re-publishing his research and titles, and for Richard Franklin of Arima Books for his support for such an initiative. I would also like to express my thanks for ideas, suggestions and encouragement from members of the Spontaneous Cases Committee of the Society for Psychical Research including Mary Rose Barrington, Barrie Colvin, John Fraser, the late Dr Peter Hallson, Dr Graham Kidd, Rita Leek, Dr John Newton, Guy Lyon Playfair and James Tacchi and especially to Steve Parsons for permission to include an abridged extract from his book *Ghostology* (2015) which is reproduced in Appendix Two.

GHOST HUNTING: A PRACTICAL GUIDE

BY ANDREW GREEN

EDITED BY ALAN MURDIE

CONTENTS

PREFACE TO THE FIRST EDITION

"It's all in the mind" is often the answer given by sceptics to the question of belief in ghosts. From knowledge and experience gained over the last thirty years I feel confident that they are right, but not in the way most scoffers imply.

Interest in the subject is rapidly increasing. With literally hundreds of case-histories being published and more popular books about ghosts appearing annually, the need for a small, non-technical guide for new investigators has become apparent. It is to be hoped that this introductory work will provide answers to some of the problems, offer fresh ideas for the amateur to consider, and encourage further investigation into the entire subject of hauntings.

The study of ghosts and associated phenomena can be interesting and rewarding, but it may not be realised how much general knowledge is required before one can seriously investigate a case of footsteps in an empty room, for example, or the phantom of a nun in an open field.

Some may feel there is no real purpose in ghost hunting. My personal view is that it enlarges the general field of knowledge, which in itself is a valid reason for any pursuit; that by helping people to understand such phenomena it can reduce the number of cases of "shattered nerves" and mental distress caused by incomprehensible "ghostly" experiences; and that it can act as an incentive to the serious study of parapsychology. It can even prove valuable from both historical and archaeological points of view: the close study by investigators of certain specific cases has uncovered previously unrecorded facts about the past.

Parapsychology (the modern term for the study of all forms of paraphysical phenomena, such as poltergeists, apparitions of the dead, phantoms of the living, ghosts of animals, and indefinable spectres) is now accepted as a serious subject for study in this country as well as in America, Russia and many parts of Europe.

Duke University of North Carolina, USA, is well known for its experiments in telepathy, and all over Russia detailed investigations of paranormal phenomena are being reported. A film was made recently featuring Alla Vinogradova who is able to move objects, under laboratory conditions, by thought alone.

That may sound incredible, but it is really just conclusive evidence of what has been known by ghost-hunters for some time: that concentrated thought, or in some cases unconscious thought, is strong enough to cause the movement of material items. This ability, which is merely an extension of telepathy, was originally termed "telekinesis" but is now known as "psychokinesis" or "PK" by investigators. It is closely associated with poltergeist activity.

Comments by Captain Ed Mitchell, the American astronaut, during a radio interview in January 1973, helped to strengthen the growing interest in psychokinesis. He told listeners of experiments in which metal had been fractured by this mental process. "It's an ability that can be trainable" he said. He believes all forms of life are connected by some means of communication, and in this connection he mentioned the receptiveness of plants to spoken threats. When attached to an electronic lie detector (a polygraph) the plants produced a definite and recordable response if spoken to harshly.

It is already being realised that many so-called ghosts are in fact phantoms of the living. In 1972 one expert told me that at least forty cases had been reported during the year, and I have personal knowledge of at least three of these, two in Sussex and the other in Kent, in England, in which much witnessed phenomena were found to be caused by individuals living a few miles away from the "haunted" site. In one of these cases, the apparition ceased immediately on the death of the unconscious operator, a retired baker. In the other, the apparition has continued to appear after the death of its "original", and has now become an "ordinary" ghost.

It is this sort of incident which offers interesting material for the potential ghost-hunter. He could well find it worth while to sort out reported incidents into various categories before deciding on what action to take. The possibility that, of the hundred or so cases each year, the majority are of ghosts of the living cannot be ruled out.

There may be other possible lines of study, of course. One might be the investigation of an unusually high number of crashes on a particular stretch of road, which may well be attributable to the sudden appearance of a ghost. Too many people are still reluctant to admit that they have witnessed a phantom, and offer what they consider a more easily acceptable reason for wrapping their car round a tree.

But there are areas on certain roads well known to be haunted, and not only by phantom figures, but by ghostly cars and even lorries. One regional office of the Automobile Association has its own phantom, and drivers in the locality are thus assured of an understanding attitude when they report they have just "knocked down a ghost".

During lectures on my experience I am sometimes asked whether it is possible to obtain a degree in psychical research or parapsychology. Strictly speaking, the answer is in the negative, though researchers can obtain a doctorate by studying this subject. One can only hope that parapsychology will become fully recognised as a science when one will be able to use the initials B.Sc (Pp) indicating a Bachelor of Parapsychology. I hope to be one of the first (albeit honorary).

Some individuals refuse to believe in things they cannot see or experience themselves. One wonders if they consider that they are a religious; and they must also find it hard to accept that they are able to see stars at night which may have been destroyed thousands of years ago. For example, one of the brightest stars in the universe, Arcturus, is forty-one light years (or twenty million million miles) away, and would therefore be visible from earth if it had been extinguished in 1923.

May I just offer a word of warning. One of the facts known about seeing a ghost is that if the witness has up to that time flatly refused to accept their existence, or has continually derided other people for believing in phantoms, he is likely to suffer a severe shock. On the other hand, if he has accepted even the mere possibility of the existence of ghosts, despite having had no personal experience of them, the new witness (though he may be somewhat surprised and alarmed at seeing the figure of a nun walk through a wall) will seldom need the attention of a doctor after his first experience of paranormal phenomena.

Just to clarify my own position: I have seen a ghost, but like so many people failed to realize that I had done so until some time later.

Good hunting.

ANDREW GREEN

CHAPTER 1

What is the proof of phenomena?

The existence of ghosts can hardly be challenged in the face of the ever mounting evidence that is published throughout the world. In Britain alone some 150 cases are reported each year and probably twice that number are never publicized.

Of the cases that reach newspapers and books about 50% relate to poltergeist activity, 25% are of long-established hauntings, and approximately 40% are of new incidents though on examination many of these may be dismissed as due to imagination, auto-suggestion or natural causes.[1]

One of the major problems is to establish proof of the authenticity of a phantom. In truly scientific terms it is practically impossible to prove one's own existence, let alone that of a non-tangible phantom. Ghosts can never be guaranteed to appear at specific times, can never be put into a laboratory to be tested under trial conditions, and cannot be persuaded to manifest themselves when required. Therefore, investigators can only set themselves specific standards by which they can judge the authenticity, or otherwise, of phenomena.

Some phenomena, such as ESP (Extra-Sensory Perception, including such aspects as clairvoyance, clairaudience and telepathy, and referred to as 'psi') can most certainly be recorded and investigated, but it rather depends on what sort of standard is set as to whether the reality of the phenomena is regarded as having been proved beyond any shadow of doubt. Clairvoyance or precognition is the mental faculty of "seeing" incidents or "pictures" in the future or at some distance away, whilst clairaudience refers to hearing sounds (usually human voices) in one's mind and is usually linked with clairvoyance. Telepathy is more popularly known as "thought transference". The latter subject has become an extremely popular one for parapsychologists, mainly because it is possible to carry out laboratory-type controlled tests and produce statistics to prove the existence of telepathy.

---

[1] Andrew Green (1996) Lecture 'Phantom Phantoms' delivered at Pyke House 10 September 1996.

Unfortunately many gullible people accept "evidence" far too easily and ignore or dismiss the possibility of fraud, mistaken observation or simple camera failure.

"Spirit photographs" are too frequently claimed as proof of existence of ghosts and life hereafter, and yet there appears to be little evidence for regarding them as such. Spirit photography was at its peak in Victorian days when Spiritualistic circles were anxious to obtain supporters. Since then, fortunately, the practice of producing obvious and not so obvious faked prints has practically disappeared.

There are, however, still many photographs that are presented as completely genuine illustrations of phenomena, ranging from unusual lights and shapes to the perfect image of a human entity appearing in a locality and at a time when the photographer was unaware of any haunting. These photographs should never be considered as proof of an "afterlife", but merely as interesting examples of instances where the photographic emulsion has recorded some image unseen by the camera operator. This situation is hardly uncommon, for the production of X-ray negatives is a daily occurrence in hospitals and industrial laboratories. Photographs taken on infra-red film and in ultra-violet light provide illustrations of many objects that the human eye can never see, and are used extensively in certain branches of archaeology, geology and industry. A few years ago considerable publicity was given to the development of a film which produced outlines of humans in localities that they had just left. This was merely super-sensitive film recording images created by body-heat.

The human eye, linked with the brain, can only register light being transmitted at certain frequencies and anything recording on film outside these is far too often treated as phenomena. As regards photographic proof, if you have taken a photograph at a haunted site it is always best to get the film processed by good printers even though you may be able to develop it yourself. There can then be no doubt of authenticity if something unusual appears on the resulting print or image. Should you be lucky and obtain what might be a paranormal image, it would be worthwhile to check with the processors and ask if they can confirm, if possible in writing, that the negative was untouched or, if digital, get the camera checked. In a particularly baffling case, you could follow the example of some experts even going so far as to submit the negatives and prints to the manufacturer of the film or of the camera or its software for assessment.

It is also necessary to beware of odd images which may be caused by photographic failures or distortions which have a mundane explanation. This is particularly so in the case of so-called 'orbs' which from the end of the 20th century numerous people have wrongly interpreted as evidence of psychic phenomena captured on film. Photographs of anomalous luminous spheres and dots have dogged ghost hunting since the mid-1990s, and informed opinion now considers them nothing more than artefacts generated by modern cameras. This has not stopped many beginners in research, as well as quite a few more experienced individuals, from proclaiming such images as evidence of ghostly presences – despite the fact that miniscule spheres of light have seldom ever been reported as such by witnesses with the unaided eye.

The phenomenon of orbs emerges from reflections of tiny particles in the air which appear on pictures because the typical flash unit of a camera in use today is much closer to the lens than with older models. Thus, those particles of dust you see in a beam of sunlight, bobbing around with air currents and 'Brownian motion' (the movement of small airborne particles caused by molecular collisions), show up as orbs when digital photography is used.

Furthermore, revealing experiments were carried out using stereoscopic cameras utilizing a Fuijifilm W1 3D digital camera, whereby matched stereo images are taken of the same view. It was found that it was not possible to capture images, as should have happened if the orb was a real and distinct object in its own right, rather than a reflection from a dust speck located close to the camera. A total of 1,870 stereo pairs of images were taken at over 20 locations in the UK and Eire, including a number of allegedly haunted sites. Some 630 orb-like images were obtained. If orbs were not reflections of particles less than 2-3 cm from the lens, then the orb should appear in both images. After exhaustive tests at 20 locations (including haunted sites) no evidence was obtained showing that orbs were independent objects, rather than reflections. However, such findings have done little to dent the will to believe in some people, though you can often create your own orb images by beating a pillow or a cushion.[2]

---

[2] Parsons, Steve (2010) Findings presented at the conference of the Society for Psychical Research in September 2010; Parsons, Steve (2010) 'Orbs!...Some Definitive Evidence That They Are Not Paranormal' by Steve Parsons in *Anomaly* the Journal of ASSAP Vol 44 November 2010. See also Carr, Philip (2009) 'Riddle of the Orbs' DVD film. Steve Parsons concludes that "...all 630 that we obtained in the survey were readily explained using the stereo photography technique. That is 0% paranormal but 100% explainable."

The recording of phantom footsteps may appear to pose a problem, for if they are in fact hallucinatory and not physical, how can their sound be electronically recorded? The answer is that if photographic emulsion may register the unseen, then magnetic tape can register electrical impulses from the atmosphere which are unheard by human ears as well as those that are heard. Videotape, used in the recording and re-recording of television programmes, collects sounds never heard by humans, for they are only created by electrical impulses in the first place.

Further comment on taped phenomena appears in Chapter 3 relating to "Raudive voices" and Electronic Voice Phenomena.

Another type of phenomena about which tangible proof is practically impossible to obtain is that of physical mediumship. The term relates to the manufacture, by means of ectoplasm issuing from any of the human orifices, of human-type figures or portions of figures, ranging from complete entities to faces, hands, or feet. Ectoplasm itself is a substance of a doubtful and mysterious nature. In a large number of cases it has been found to be cheese-cloth, sometimes regurgitated by the medium; in one séance the "face of the departed" was found to consist of lavatory paper stuck together. The exposure of these crude frauds, together with the stringent conditions laid down by serious investigators, has had its effect on the number of physical mediums available.

One of the other problems experienced by new researchers into the field of physical mediumship is the rule imposed by the medium herself at the séance that neither she, nor the ectoplasm, be touched during the materialisation, and that the phenomena may only take place in very dim light. Nevertheless it must be admitted that if a person is in a trance in a subdued light, a sudden change of strong illumination, or grasping what might be a physical part of her body, could certainly be liable to cause damage, mental as well as physical. Infra-red equipment would therefore be needed to record the outcome of a sitting; fortunately today modern infrared cameras are inexpensive compared with the past and these experiments can be conducted cheaply and simply, although the installation of them may in any case not be acceptable to the medium. For proper investigation in this field, equipment for testing and measuring the physiological state of the medium would be necessary, operated by trained and medically qualified practitioners.

Despite the problems regarding the establishing of the reality of ectoplasm, it appears nevertheless in a few cases to have been a genuine substance, strong enough to be moulded into shapes of human hands and feet from which plaster casts have been taken; however, the rarity of such cases today under controlled conditions inevitably encourages a sceptical approach. Some success has been claimed with laboratory testing individuals who have been the centre of poltergeist activity, but it is rare to have the necessary support and cooperation available from both scientists and poltergeist agents and their families willing to act as research volunteers.

Incidentally the Society for Psychical Research once offered a reward of £1,000 for anyone producing physical phenomena to their satisfaction under conditions laid down by them. The offer was withdrawn a few years ago, but an American University still offers an even greater incentive – £80,000 – for the production of unequivocal evidence for life after death. In the face of such attractive offers, there may well be room for doubt concerning the genuine nature of many mediumistic performances.

Other physical phenomena stated to take place during séances include the movement of specially designed trumpets, tables, tambourines and lights, all of which, according to one leading Spiritualist, are moved by "ectoplasmic rods". Despite the much publicised statement that sitters at séances must be "in accord with the medium" or at least not antagonistic, I have found it possible to develop a trance medium, in the course of six months, to a standard that a leading Spiritualistic medium in Middlesex admitted to me would have taken four or five years to accomplish under "normal" conditions. The lady concerned went into a trance at the third meeting and was talking in "direct voice communication" at the fifth meeting. This was achieved in a small sitting room illuminated with a 200 watt bulb without the paraphernalia of crucifixes or the necessity of hymns.

A comment received from an "entity" whilst the medium was in a trance was that she had "come to the meeting as a result of our combined thoughts". This phrase was practically identical to that in a letter written to me by one of the sitters the day before the séance, which had not at that time reached me.

What was extremely interesting was the amount of information obtained from the "entity" concerning the early days of Christian Science. She claimed that when "on earth" she was a "close companion" of Mary Baker Eddy, the founder of the particular religion. Although the medium herself had practically no knowledge of Christian Science, her husband, the writer of the letter, admitted months afterwards that he had read most (if not all) of the material that was supplied through his wife.

5

One of the group involved was a sceptic, another antagonistic to the very idea of life after death, and the lady herself had to be reassured fairly frequently that we would not become Spiritualists. (Let me hasten to reassure readers that I have absolutely nothing against the work of Spiritualists and in fact, I have often stated if a law should be imposed to force the population to join a religious sect I would immediately align myself with the Spiritualist Church, for I believe that it is the only religious body to offer tangible assistance to people seeking some form of truth whatever that might be).

To return to the question of proof. What constitutes proof of phenomena in light of ever-increasing scientific knowledge?

One must consider the problems involved. It is very difficult to obtain tangible evidence of a ghost, although such evidence might be obtained in the case of a physical manifestation produced by a medium, if one could find a medium prepared to accept the necessary conditions. Evidence of poltergeist activity is obtainable in many cases, and telepathy tests may yield encouragingly concrete results if one sets reliable standards, which may have to vary as tests proceed. As this work is aimed at the potential ghost hunter such subjects as dreams, astrology, witchcraft and palmistry are not included, though in some instances, of course, some of these may be associated with individual cases of haunting.

Proof of a haunting, as far as the parapsychologist is concerned, can be evaluated according to the credibility of the witness and other factors which will be dealt with in due course. Basically, all one can hope for is sufficient personal evidence, linked with historical detail, recordings and perhaps photographic material and documentation, to provide a strong case for a paranormal incident. (Never use the terms "super-normal" or "supernatural", for both imply "greater than normality". Paranormal or paraphysical are the correct descriptions, defining the phenomena as "irregular" normality.) Another word, increasingly used in psychology is 'anomalous'; it should be remembered that many 'normal' aspects of the brain and mind have yet to explained before we come to psychic powers.

It should be realized that what might be regarded as conclusive proof or evidence by one individual might not be acceptable to another who uses different standards and methods and who might be biased at the outset. Many people are still over-sceptical, others are too gullible and will accept any case which confirms their own established beliefs. Unfortunately, there are some individuals who refuse to accept proof of any sort, especially if it is likely to authenticate something they do not wish to believe in, or which would disturb their mental attitude, however well-documented the proof may be. The interpretation of facts is, and always will be, a major problem to researchers.

If you wish to pursue a case to a satisfactory conclusion and perhaps then submit it to a learned body, then show your "case-file of proof" to a serious sceptic, but not one who will dismiss it out of hand. If s/he expresses doubt, find out exactly why s/he regards the material as inconclusive, and what type of evidence would be personally acceptable to him/her. Also, re-read the case yourself with, if possible, a detached outlook, and seriously consider whether it satisfies *you*.

The notion that investigators might manufacture or accept doubtful evidence in order to achieve a positive or negative case would obviously invalidate the entire investigation and make nonsense of its purpose. Unfortunately, some ghost-hunters are prepared to ignore advice and are inclined to take the easy way out by accepting reports without checking them. The true investigator should question everything, including information in documents or appearing on-line. To produce near professional standards professional methods must be employed. Lawyers demand proof of a death or a birth by means of an attested certificate. So should the ghost-hunter, especially in view of what has been said earlier concerning phantoms of the living. Copies of such documents are easily obtained and add strength to any argument, as would sworn statements by witnesses, although these are rarely requested and seldom received.

Sources of information regarding haunted sites may cause an initial problem. How does one find a ghost?

There are various methods, but the close study of newspapers and magazines in the hope of finding a recent report can be tedious and slow. A better idea would be to contact a newspaper-cutting agency and order a supply of relevant cuttings for a period of say three, six or twelve months, or a quantity of 100, or conduct detailed on-line searches via the internet.

I would suggest, however, that the best method is to join a society or group associated with such matters and study some of the latest books on ghosts, titles of which are given later. Some of these publications provide details of the locations of haunted sites, and one or two even provide the names of recent witnesses of apparitions.

I have been seriously asked if it is just at Christmas time that ghosts appear. Let me assure readers that phantoms have been witnesses at all times of the year, at all hours of the day and night and in all types of situations. They have been seen in open fields and closed laboratories, in derelict private houses and in audience-packed theatres, in castles and in pre-fabs, in factories, and even, in a couple of cases, semi-public lavatories.

It is interesting to note that there are very few cases of genuine haunted graveyards, and even fewer instances where ghosts are seen at exactly midnight, although admittedly about 50% of new cases occur at night. Indeed, there may be a time of day effect with some studies suggesting that the frequency of sightings increases as the day goes on into night-time with a peak between midnight and 4 A.M. This suggests a possible link with dreaming and dream-like states, and brain chemistry at night.[3] Clanking chains are completely "out" and, as far as I know, moaning spectres dragging their ball and chain have not been seen since Charles Dickens's time, even if then.

Ghosts can be found wherever people live, die, work or play.

If you wish to start from scratch, as it were, a letter to your local paper may create interest and provoke some response, perhaps including details of a little-known and previously unpublicized haunt. Then you need only follow up the lead by contacting the informant or visiting the site.

One point that should be considered is the period involved. Are you interested in "historical" and much-publicized ghosts such as those at the Tower of London or Glamis Castle, or would you prefer the more recently experienced cases where it may be possible to meet witnesses? Obviously, for the purpose of real study and investigation it is preferable to concentrate on the most recent incidents, of which people's memories will still be clear.

Unfortunately, but understandably, large organised societies specialising in the study of the paranormal are to be found only in the main population centres, so one idea which may be worth considering is to form an investigation group yourself, especially if you know some friends willing to join you in your investigations. A letter to the local paper or a chat with the editor could well result in much valuable assistance in launching such a

[3] MacKenzie, Andrew (1982) *Ghosts and Apparitions*; Roney Dougal, Serena (1989) Recent findings relating to the possible role of the pineal gland in affecting psychic ability. *Journal of the Society for Psychical Research* 55, 313-328.

project. With the internet it is much easier to establish contact with like-minded people at a distance, including internationally.

Some members of the group will naturally wish to pursue one line of investigation whilst others will prefer to study another aspect, but after a few months of settling down a society of this nature could become a valuable group of dedicated investigators. It would be wise to attempt to provide a programme of activities for the year in order that interest can be maintained, and I would recommend that at least one of the group should be a member of the well-known organisations, such as the Society for Psychical Research, the Parapsychology Association and the Association for the Study of Anomalous Phenomena or the College of Psychic Studies. To add prestige, it might be wise to offer such a member an executive position in the group.

Close attention to detail is essential when keeping the society's records and reports, for, if such a group is to achieve its purpose and attain a reputation for honesty and integrity, published material regarding investigations might be a source of funds for the purchase of equipment.

Before you proceed with forming any group, however, it will be helpful to examine your personal outlook. If you are prepared to accept that ghosts are "spirits of the dead" without any question or any basis of evidence – remembering that the concept of a "spirit" has no place in the world of science – then this book is probably not for you. But may I refer the practising Christian to *Spiritualism* by K.N. Ross, published by the Society for the Promotion of Christian Knowledge, in which it is stated that "Christianity" has no quarrel with psychical research conducted under suitable conditions and it is shallow materialism which dismissed the paranormal and miraculous as being all hallucination or coincidence; another useful work is *Deliverance: Psychic Disturbances and Occult Involvement.*[4]

---

[4] Perry, Michael (1996, 2012) *Deliverance: Psychic Disturbance and Occult Involvement*. UK. Society for the Promotion of Christian Knowledge.

CHAPTER 2

Personal outlook and experimentation

Before carrying out any ghost-hunting you should seriously consider your reasons for doing so. Is it that you have witnessed some phenomena yourself, do you know someone who has been disturbed at seeing a phantom, or has some book you have read recently sparked off a greater interest in the subject?

Then be warned. If you wish to take up the subject of parapsychology seriously, and to carry out investigations in any other way would be foolish, then you must realize that there is a lot to learn, and a lot of time may be involved for which there is little financial return.

Consider what time you are planning to devote to this new hobby, for the majority of hours should probably be spent in study. It is often not realised how vast a literature exists on psychical research and parapsychology, in many languages. Books on specific aspects of this wide-ranging subject can be obtained from libraries, both those of the local council and those of the learned societies (if you are a member), or from specialist book shops and services on-line. A small question, although an important one, is whether you should buy books or borrow them. A lot depends on the book itself, the costs and your own finances, of course, but if it is the type that provides information you may need at short notice in the future then you should obviously purchase it if you can, for not to have vital information readily available could cause quite serious problems.

It may be desirable to examine your own religious outlook, for this could colour your attitude.

It is essential for any investigator to adopt an open mind, and to be prepared to sift and search and question everything. If you have any preconceived ideas about hauntings and ghosts, re-consider their logicality. On the other hand never dismiss the possibility of the existence of apparitions; not only does this attitude resemble that of the proverbial ostrich but it could result in some unpleasant experiences if you come face to face with a ghost. According to some polls, at least one person in five (nearly ten million in this country) has experienced some psychic phenomena and one in ten has seen a ghost. One point, although an obvious one, must be made. An intangible phenomenon that cannot be felt physically, is unable to move objects, and is not equipped with vocal chords or any other physical attributes, cannot harm anything or anyone. This refers only to the normal ghost, phantom, spectre, or whatever you wish to call it. Poltergeist activity, which is most certainly not in the same category, although very occasionally it is experienced at the same time as a haunting, has been known to cause some mental stress as well as a certain amount of physical pain due to an object being thrown at a witness. [5]

It is vital therefore for the potential researcher, who must be well balanced in outlook, to adopt a rational approach to the whole subject. Fanaticism is a major form of neurosis and there are too many fanatics as it is. Those suffering from any mental anxiety or problems would be well advised to forget all about taking-up ghost hunting as an interest. It should always be remembered that it is not always possible to control phenomena in a poltergeist case, and this could become disturbing.

The serious study of paranormal phenomena need not interfere with or have any detrimental effect on any faith. In some cases I believe it has strengthened some people's faith whilst the opinion that "it is unnatural and merely dabbling with the Devil" can be offset by the fact that many members of the established Church have been active researchers in the field. One chairman of the Unitarian Society for Psychical Studies was the Rev. John Robbins, FHA, FRSH; the Rev C. Drayton Thomas was a well known author of books about ghosts; and there are numerous religious attitudes and beliefs represented by members of the world authority, the Society for Psychical Research, whose President in 1912 was the Rt Rev. Bishop W. Boyd Carpenter, DD. Special courses are now being held in the Anglican Church for priests wishing to assist in cases of hauntings.

The established Churches are therefore beginning to accept parapsychology as a respectable activity seriously searching for truth. Admittedly it is comforting to believe that one lives after death and people will continue to accept this idea with or without any evidence, but I would prefer to experience proof, assuming that such proof could be established.

Before pursuing the investigation of a case I would suggest that a major requirement is an understanding of telepathy. Although telepathy is still a matter of controversy and to some people remains unproven there is, I feel,

[5] Examples of survey evidence include – *Phantasms of the Living* (1886) by Gurney, E, Myers, F, & Podmore, F; the Sidgwick Case collection (1888) by the SPR; various SPR surveys 1920 – 1990; *Journal of Paraphysics* surveys 1967-1974; SPR Spontaneous Cases survey 2007; Gauld Alan & Cornell, Anthony (1979) in *Poltergeists*. UK Routledge

sufficient tangible evidence and personal experience to accept that thought transference does occur. Whether or not one can accept this, a study of the subject is strongly advisable.

Fig. 1 - ZENER CARDS

It might well be worthwhile to carry out some experiments by means of Zener cards or similar devices. Zener cards (fig, I), were originally designed by the renowned Dr J.B. Rhine of Duke University for the specific purpose of carrying out such experiments, although almost any type of object can be chosen for telepathy tests. Photographs, playing cards, Scrabble blocks, Lexicon cards or the newly designed "clock card" which illustrates a clock face on which the solitary hand points to one of the hourly positions, are all suitable. Even fingers have been used in some tests, the sender holding up one or more digits for the guesser to try to establish the correct number. A wide range of possible tests have been attempted internationally which may suggest a power to communicate information, thoughts and sensations.[6]

Whatever objects are used it is vital that accurate records be kept if anything is to be achieved, and pre-printed score sheets can be devised for this purpose are also available from the SPR. It is quite easy to compile one's own, and a typical score sheet is shown as figure 2.

---

[6] See Rhine, J.B. (1947) *New Frontiers of the Mind*; West D.J. (1963) *Psychical Research Today*; Cardena, Etzel. Lynn, Steven J. and Krippner. Stanley (2000) *Varieties of Anomalous Experience*. USA American Psychological Association

Telepathy may be an ability which is shared with some animals, with cases of dogs which seem to know when their owner is coming home and with cats which seem to have a sensitivity as to when they may be about to be taken for a trip to the vet – with a result that they go into hiding (many vets' surgeries have reported the difficulty with cat-owners keeping appointments because the cat has suddenly absented itself from the home). Earlier experiments were carried out on cats, in an effort to establish whether it was possible by "thought control" to cause the animals to move to a specific saucer of milk. Given a choice of five identical containers, statistics seemed to imply that it was possible.[7]

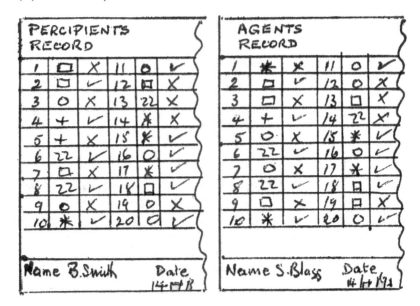

Fig. 2 - SCORE SHEETS FOR TELEPATHY TESTS

Distance is no object. It seems that telepathy operates equally well between Chelsea and Melbourne as between the front and back rooms of a small private house. But it should be remembered that there seems to be similarity between failing, by concentrating too intensely, to achieve a telepathic link, and trying unsuccessfully to see a ghost, so don't be disappointed: there are not many ghost-hunters, if any, who have seen ghosts when purposely looking for them.

---

[7] Sheldrake, Rupert (1999) *Dogs Who Know When Their Owners Are Coming Home*. Hutchison Publishers.

The method of carrying out tests for "ESP", as it is commonly but incorrectly termed (for Extra-Sensory Perception covers more than just telepathy), involves at least four people. One acts as the sender or agent, another as the receiver or percipient, and the two others as recorders.

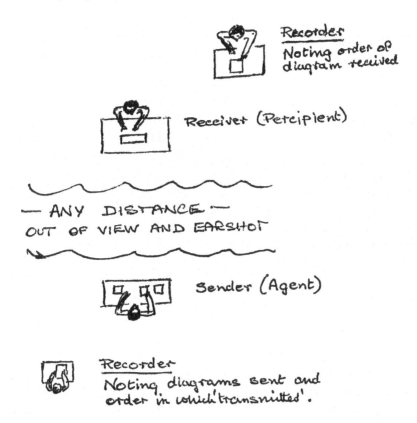

Fig. 3 - TELEPATHY TESTS

The agent and percipient must not be in view of each other or within earshot, for the slightest sound, such as breathing (which can be significant), may be considered a signal and invalidate the experiment (see fig. 3). For sophisticated tests electrical equipment incorporating push-buttons, buzzers and/or light signals between agent and percipient can be used, but for normal trials only pen and paper, and of course the objects, are required.

Assuming that cards are used, the pack is shuffled by one of the recorders and passed face down to the agent. At a pre-arranged signal (a specific time, a ring on the bell or a buzzer) the sender picks up the first card, looks at it and puts it down, creating a separate pile for checking the order later, The next card is picked up, looked at and put down until every design is "sent".

No deep concentration is called for and I feel the time spent looking at each object or card should certainly not exceed two seconds, but obviously there must be some prior arrangement made with the percipient as to the time actually "sending" each design. Perhaps the recorder could tap or ring a bell after each period, or if electrical equipment is used then a buzzer could act as the signal for "next please".

The percipient, who should start the tests with a blank mind, either writes down the design that he is picking up or calls out to the recorder "square", "lines", "nine o'clock" or "G" (as the case may be), indicating the outlines. An alternative method would be the use of electrically operated buttons each illustrating some design, but this set-up could be expensive and no more accurate. Another simpler scheme is for the percipient merely to point to the designs, which would have been supplied before the trials commenced. One easy method to attain a receptive state of mind is mentally to picture a white sheet or a blank cinema screen.

The majority of experts seem to accept that odds better than 20 to 1 against is the criterion for significant results. In other words, chance expectation is five hits per run of 25. A successful guess is known as a "hit". Thus what experts term as a "high level of significance" relates to a small value of probability.

Tests of this nature can prove extremely interestingly or quite boring, depending on the participant's outlook. It should be remembered that both parties are inclined to lose interest after a certain time and this will be evident in the results. Therefore batches of tests should be concluded immediately the allotted time is reached, say one hour, or after four times through the pack.

Once a batch test is completed both recorders compare their lists, and by checking with each other and the order of the objects themselves can ascertain the number of correct hits and hence the occurrence or otherwise of telepathy. To provide variety during sessions it might be advisable to alternate functions among the members of the group, recorders becoming in turn agents and percipients.

Don't get disheartened. Some telepathy tests have lasted for years involving literally thousands of trials and hundreds of people.

In a BBC radio broadcast in 1973 Captain Mitchell, the American astronaut, spoke of the random number generator which had been designed by Dr Helmut Schmidt to enable people to "guess" numbers before they were produced. Dr Tart of the University of California also produced a similar unit and others have been made in this country. John Cutten of the Society for Psychical Research produced a design for an electronic apparatus for this purpose some years ago, and a couple of other such units are already in use. Captain Mitchell also stated that "very little training was needed to achieve a score above chance", but some people can quite obviously achieve high scores without special training. This research was later followed by the American military which spent 22 years in endeavouring to test and develop telepathy and 'remote viewing' for security and espionage purposes, the so-called Stargate programme which is detailed in now declassified documents and books.[8]

From the 1980s, in parapsychology laboratories processes have been automated with a technique known as the 'Ganzfeld' test where a relaxed subject suffers a degree of sensory isolation, having his/her eyes covered whilst wearing headphones blocking out external sounds delivering white noise to the ears. In this state of sensory deprivation, the subject is encouraged to record mental impressions that may come spontaneously in a relaxed state, whilst a second person attempts to transmit an image or series of images by telepathy (the images may be a selection of video clips and films). The process may be fully automated so that there is no human interaction between the two subjects.[9] Results seem to indicate that relaxed and altered states of consciousness are conducive to receiving psychic impressions, as with the large number of apparitions seen when people are in a state of relaxation or in bed.

It will be found that some people are better than others at "guessing" correctly at certain times, so vary the times, and vary also the method and objects. The next session may produce better figures or even what appear to be unusual statistics.

---

[8] May, Edwin and Marwaha, Sonali (2014) *Anomalous Cognition: Remote Viewing Research and Theory.* USA. MacFarland; May, Edwin C., Rubel Victor and Auerbach, Loyd (2014) *ESP Wars: East and West: An account of the Military Use of Psychic Espionage as Narrated by the Key Russian and American Players.* Create Space Independent Publisher Platform.

[9] Smith, R., Tremmel, L. and Honorton, C., "A comparison of psi and weak sensory influences on Ganzfeld mentation" (1976) In: Morris, J. D., Roll, W. G. and Morris, R. L. (eds), *Research in Parapsychology 1975.* New Jersey. Metchuen- Scarecrow Press.

Many tests carried out may appear at first scrutiny to indicate a score of hits so much lower that the operation of chance would produce as to imply error in recording results. Re-examination may show that the percipient was "receiving" designs one or two cards before the agent had touched them. This is not as unusual as it may sound, and is recognised as precognitive.

Another aspect is the sense of being stared at, whereby people seem to be able to tell when they are being observed by another person, even in situations of sensory shielding. This sense of knowing when someone is thinking or observing you is a long-standing folkloric belief which now seems to be supported by some amount of experimental evidence by Rupert Sheldrake and others. Other interesting lines of enquiry have been people who seem to know when someone is about to telephone them and a connectedness which occurs between biological twins.[10]

Fig. 4 - SEEING A GHOST – SKETCH PLAN OF THE INCIDENT

The value of experiments of this nature is that they tend to indicate that telepathy *does* exist, and this fact must obviously be taken into account when "in the field". For example, one case occurred where five people were involved. Four saw the ghost, but the fifth, despite descriptions and details of its exact locality being supplied, was unable to see the apparition.

This illustration (fig.4), shows the exact positions of all witnesses at the time. All were facing roughly towards the apparition of "a woman in white".

---

[10] Playfair, Guy (1998, 2012) *Twin Telepathy*. UK. White Crow Books.

Witness E failed to see it, the descriptions given by C and D tallied, A saw it as expected, but witness B described the figure as being "several feet away on her left" whereas the other three placed its position as only two feet from her right hand side. This strongly suggests, at least to me, that the witness nearest the apparition was only viewing it through the eyes of one of the others, especially as she stated she could see "its back view". From her position at least a semi-profile should have been visible.

Witness E, incidentally, was in a hurry and concentrating on getting to work on time, whereas the other four admitted that they were not thinking of anything in particular. Here then we have differing states of mind, three receptive (one super-receptive to telepathy), and one engrossed and far from receptive at that particular time. Telepathy should therefore never be ignored as a possible answer when a phenomenon is witnessed by more than one person at an identical moment in time. It would be interesting, in this connection to include a non-English speaking individual in telepathy tests. Questions would then arise as to whether the image of the word is being transmitted, of whether the *sense* of the words is being received.

Not only can visual phenomena be "transmitted" for (as is generally accepted) any emotional reaction, such as fear or adoration, can be transferred from one person to another. This becomes very obvious in crowds and large gatherings such as political meetings, in theatres or even in sports events. I recall one incident where I "picked up" extreme fright from a man standing beside me who could obviously see a ghost only a few feet from him; on another occasion I acted as the "transmitter", causing my companion extreme alarm because of what I was witnessing.

Other forms of experimentation can indicate the unreliability of witnesses. Show a group of people a number of objects for a short time and then ask the individuals for detailed descriptions of what they have seen. The variety of replies can sometimes be amusing, but is hardly ever accurate.

This human failing was emphasised in an incident in a police college. A group of senior police officers undergoing examination for promotion were being marched from one lecture hall to another for a new session. As they were marching down the path, a man came towards them and passed in the building they had just left. He was wearing a trilby hat, a dark grey suit, and black shoes, and was carrying an umbrella in one hand and a large model panda toy in the other.

Immediately the officers arrived in the lecture hall they were asked what they had seen on their short journey. Practically all mentioned the man, some giving a perfect description of the figure but only one of the sixteen noted the toy, and he described it as "a teddy bear".

There could be many reasons for this apparently poor standard of observation. The policemen's minds were perhaps still occupied with details of the lecture they had just been given; or they were mentally preparing themselves for the next talk; they had not expected to see a man carrying a toy panda in a police college and therefore were unable to register the unusual picture, or possibly they did not wish to suggest they had seen anything so peculiar. Many more examples of this failure to notice things may be given.[11]

If police executives can react in this way, how can one expect a person who has just seen a ghost, perhaps for the first time, to provide a full and detailed description to a complete stranger? Nevertheless, that is often just what the ghost-hunter must try to obtain.

Inconsistencies and sometimes downright contradictions will be encountered in the statements people make. There really is "none so queer as folk". In a recent poll several people claimed that they didn't believe in ghosts and then immediately provided details of phantoms that they themselves had witnessed. Even a curator of a museum admitted to me that he had experienced some phenomena, yet refused to believe it.

This attitude of non-acceptance of personal evidence is frequently associated with rather introverted personalities who are afraid of being laughed at, and immediately they realise the interviewer is talking about the matter seriously they often admit that the really "had to believe it, but it's silly isn't it?". So never show any amusement at descriptions given by witnesses even if they themselves are giggling. Ghosts are not normally funny and laughing at details being given by someone trying to hide his fright will nearly always halt the flow of information and will certain affect the authenticity of the incident. The witness, realizing that the interviewer is finding the tale amusing, will embellish and invent in order to keep the interviewer satisfied. It really is surprising the number of people who, when questioned, will offer an answer that they think is the one the interviewer wants to hear, regardless of the fact that it may well be untrue.

[11] Holt, Nicola, J, Simmond-More, Luke, David, French, Christopher C. *Anomalistic Psychology* (2012) Basingstoke, UK. Palgrave Macmillan.

Another small and amusing game which gives further evidence of human fallibility is to whisper a phrase or sentence to someone in a crowd, perhaps at a party, and ask him to pass on the message. The phrase which eventually returns to you can be guaranteed to be nothing like the one you originally created. Hearsay evidence is therefore subject to doubt and is always open to question.

If one wishes to practice parapsychology a basic understanding of psychology, or at least an appreciation of human characteristics and mental patterns, is naturally desirable.

Why do people act as they do? Are there certain types of people who are really afraid of ghosts? Why are others not subject to this fear? If it is fear of the unknown which creates a feeling of unease and apprehension then why not make the unknown known? This should be the aim of the ghost hunter.

Are there certain types of people who actually witness phenomena? As has been pointed out earlier, at least one in five people in this country admit to having experienced psychic phenomena of some sort during their lifetime. That is roughly 9 million incidents in the last 50 years, or over 165,000 a year. Many of these cases relate only to dreams apparently foretelling the future, a telepathic incident or an experience of "feeling I have been here before".

One line of study has suggested that people who are inclined to see apparitions have a family history of epilepsy, or its associated disorders. Another investigator states that if a person has once witnessed the appearance of a ghost then he or she is more likely to have another similar experience.[12]

One factor seems clear, and that is there is no specific age for seeing ghosts. A child of eight is just as likely to see a phantom as a person of eighty. Some years ago, however, I carried out a survey in an effort to establish whether children were more likely to see apparitions than adults.

The total number of children questioned was 125, ranging between the ages of 6 and 12 years. Of the 125, 65 (over 50%) described human figures that they had seen, in some cases several times, but which were not apparently visible to their parents. 27 of the 65 descriptions were found to match those of people who had once occupied the child's current home, though

---

[12] Green, Andrew in a lecture at Pyke House College, Battle, Sussex on 10 September 1996.

unfortunately I was unable to establish if more than nine of the 27 people described were deceased.

Results like these may help to explain why more phantoms are not seen. The reason for this seems to be the effect of parental control superimposing itself on the child's receptive mind. The majority of parents, rightly or wrongly, will either persuade the child that it is wrong or bad to see what his parents cannot see, or will impose conformity by insisting that to "see ghosts" is "naughty and telling stories". This attitude may well affect developing imagination as well as blanking out the child's receptive powers. It is possible that more enlightened parents, by *not* taking this attitude and allowing their off-spring to continue witnessing, talking and playing with "an unseen guest", create an environment suitable for the development of mediumistic qualities.

Another result of this small survey is the suggestion that ghosts are "there to be seen at all times". Perhaps one day a more thorough investigation into this particular aspect of ghost-hunting will be carried out.

Domestic animals can also be used in some experimentation work, for they seem in general to be far more sensitive to atmosphere and apparitions than humans. There are many cases where a dog or a cat has obviously watched something that was invisible to its owners. Could this faculty be similar to that of the child whose receptive mind has been allowed to develop unhindered by parental intervention?

In some instances, the animal is obviously scared by what it sees: why? It is perhaps that apparitions have no scent and yet appear, to the animal, to be acting in a human fashion? Dogs sometimes adopt quite frightening attitudes in the presence of a phantom – snarling, bristling and slavering as if temporarily insane. And yet there are numerous occasions where the creature obviously accepts the appearance of the phantom and acts as if it were completely human.

Perhaps the major problem is here is how to investigate the effect of the animals' experience. Despite some pet-lovers beliefs, there is little resemblance between the mind of a cat or a dog and that of a human. True, one can teach a dog tricks, but it is much more difficult to train a cat. Possibly this implies that the cat has a higher intelligence quotient as well as a greater measure of independence and individuality.

As mentioned earlier, it appears possible to communicate by thought with some domestic pets to a limited degree under laboratory conditions. This fact could well lead to experiments with animals in known haunted sites and locations.

An interesting experiment was conducted by the parapsychologist, the late Robert Morris. Then at Duke University, he visited a reputedly house in Kentucky containing a room where a murder had been committed. Tests took place using different animals, a dog, a cat, a white rat and a rattlesnake. The dog came just two feet into the room before snarling at its owner and backing out of the door and refused to re-enter, despite cajoling by its owner. The cat was carried into the room and at the same point leapt up on to her owner and then jumped to the floor and orientated herself towards an empty chair. For the next few minutes the cat "spent several minutes hissing and spitting at the empty chair" until taken out of the room. There was no discernible reaction from the behaviour of the rat when it was brought in but the rattle-snake immediately assumed an attack posture focusing on the same chair. None of the animals reacted in a similar way in any other room in the house.[13]

Other experiments carried out have indicated that not only cats and chickens could influence a machine which switched on a heater, but also embryonic chickens – eggs, in fact. There is, of course, the possibility that the researcher himself was responsible for the psychokinesis – the thought power – and this is difficult to establish.

Although it may not be immediately obvious to the uninitiated, there is often a connection between telepathy and what occurs in séances. Bearing this in mind, further trials could be carried out using an apparatus such as the ouija board or planchette. It should never be assumed that the so-called messages are anything but written evidence of telepathy, or the expression of sub-conscious thoughts of the sitters or participants.

Descriptions of equipment are given in a later chapter. Both the ouija board and the planchette can easily be made by any handyman, though commercial models are available. A prototype of the detector model of the planchette designed by the author has been used satisfactorily to indicate when the unit was being pushed.

---

[13] Morris, Robert (1971) 'An experimental approach to the survival problem' *Theta* No. 34:33

An amusing variation of card-guessing tests for ESP is to reproduce either a completed drawing or one being executed out of sight of the percipient. Problems obviously arise, however, when attempts are made to decide how successful the results are, so it may be necessary to call upon the services of an unbiased judge. A couple of examples from a "picture-transferring test" are shown in fig. 5. It is up to the reader to decide on the impressiveness of the results.

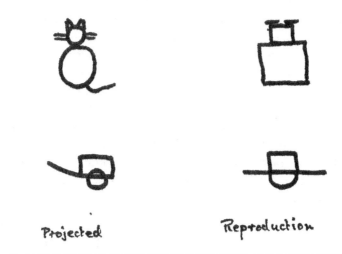

Projected   Reproduction

Fig. 5 - ILLUSTRATION TWO SETS OF DRAWINGS FROM A TELEPATHY EXPERIMENT

CHAPTER 3

Some definitions

What is a ghost? The popular belief is that it is the earth-bound spirit of someone who has died and for certain reasons continues to haunt the locality until persuaded to "pass on". Like many investigators I have been unable to find any evidence for this idea because I am not convinced that "spirits" whatever they may be, exist, but this is of course only my personal view.

In order to provide a definition of a ghost it is necessary to categorize various phantoms into their types.

Apparitions of the Deceased

This classification is really dealt with under other headings, but it should be pointed out that cases cannot be correctly categorized as apparitions of the deceased if the witness knew the person concerned was dead, for auto-suggestion and imagination may be too powerful and over-rule the probability of a paranormal incident.

To be treated as genuine, the apparition would also have to be completely unknown to the percipient and recognised by him only after an illustration has been shown to him or a full description given. This would eliminate cases where a witness reports that he has "just seen the ghost of old Aunt Maude", for example, and in fact disposes of a lot of cases of popular hauntings.

Sometimes it is believed that a phantom has imparted a message to a witness, but I must emphasise that modern apparitions never converse. Any "message" will usually prove to be the uppermost thought in the mind of the phantom's "original" at the time of the phantom's creation. Only if the information was solely known to the dead person (the originator of the ghost) will such a case be accepted as paranormal. If the witness already knew the basic details of the information received mentally or aurally, the incident cannot be treated as genuinely paranormal. And proving the facts in such a case may cause problems.

Appearance of a ghost

What does a ghost look like? This question is often put to me, but it is one on which it is not possible to generalize.

It may look like a dog or a lady in a white gown, a blue donkey or a monk. It may appear as solid as any human or insubstantial as steam. It may appear to be a complete person or a gliding pillar of mist. Sometimes it appears to be so normal that it is presumed to be a human or animal until it walks through a wall or just vanishes into thin air.

In three case I heard of in 1972 the phantoms were of men's trousers. One case was in a private house in Surrey, another in a shop in Devon, and the third in an open field in Gloucestershire. All these incidents I suspect are of "old ghosts" which have not been witnessed for many years, and the trousers are all that is left of the complete image; or perhaps the top portion of the figure was hidden from view when it was originally created, possibly by a strong light in the indoor cases or by a tree in the incident in the field. Never let it be said that the ghost hunter fails to look for a logical explanation of any phenomena!

Crisis Apparitions (and those of the living)

This is a variety of "true ghost" which is witnessed more often in wartime than in any other. The witness sees a phantom of a friend or a relative who is at that moment undergoing a traumatic experience or is nearing death some distance away. This could be a few feet, but is more often many miles from the witness.

In many cases the phantom is a man or a boy who is seen by his wife or mother. There are several reports which suggest that it is not unusual for clairaudience to be experienced at the same time as the appearance of the apparition. The figure is seen and accompanied by a mental message, which may appear to be the name of the witness.

The apparition is caused, it is believed, by the agent or sender at the very moment of stress thinking of the person closest to him, perhaps calling out, physically or mentally, to the friend or relative in question. For example, a soldier being wounded on a battle-field might be thinking of his mother just before he died, or a man knocked down in a car crash might think immediately of his wife. It has been known for such a phantom to be seen by an unrelated witness, and this could be caused by the agent's mind concentrating for a second on his home or former home, or a specific object in a room, perhaps a chair or a fireplace. The agent would of course not know that a stranger was occupying the area to which his mind had wandered.

Another type of ghost of the living can occur when the mind of the transmitter or agent is concentrated by intense emotion, such as rage. I knew of one such case in Kent, where the ghost of a farmer was seen several times at two o'clock in the morning standing on a balcony "shouting obscenities and demanding that "the damned man go back home."

This incident, experienced by a technologist and his wife on several occasions, was caused by a tenant farmer who had been resident in the house some years previously, and who had conceived an intense and utter hatred towards the landlord, who had purchased the house "over his head" and let it without any reference to the sitting tenant. A few hours later the farmer, by now roaring drunk and filled with anger, had clambered out on the balcony and created the performance that was to be observed for a period of several weeks two years later.

The image of the phantom was transparent and the railings of the balcony could be seen through the apparition, but it was clear enough in outline and colouring to be identified. One can perhaps imagine the feelings of the witnesses when they were later introduced to the "ghost" in person. Once the phenomena had been explained the phantom was never seen again.

Another case where personal knowledge can authenticate the record occurred in Sussex. An old bakery which had been operated for several generations by a local family was sold. Shortly after moving in, the wife of the new owner reported that she could "feel the presence of someone in the bakery". This phenomenon developed to a stage where doors were seen to open, baking equipment move and the woman felt "the entity push past her on numerous occasions". Both her husband and son began to experience the haunting. Disturbed, they visited the former owners in an attempt to find out more about the ghost, but were assured that the premises were not haunted and never had been during the entire occupation of the original family.

It was noticed during the visit that the "old man" had said little during the conversation and "seemed half asleep most of the time".

The incidents continued unabated for some two years and they had a very disturbing effect on the peace of mind of the family involved. Suddenly, one Tuesday, "the place seemed different". The phenomena had ceased and have never been experienced again.

Is it really surprising to learn that the old man died suddenly that Tuesday morning? Having retired from the business he had nothing to occupy his mind apart from recollecting his days spent producing high-quality bread. He would visualize himself back in the shop kneading the dough at a certain time, cutting and shaping it, then putting it on to the trays and sliding the unbaked loaves into the oven. This would coincide with the times at which his successor was carrying out identical operations.

In this particular case phantom actions were observed, although no phantom was seen. This phenomenon was not caused by any crisis, but it must still fall into the "living ghost" category, as must many others of a similar nature.

A well-known case from the 19th century, although not well-authenticated, was that of a French schoolmistress, Mlle. Emille Sagee, who was observed several times in two places at the same time over many years. On more than one occasion her double was reputedly seen within a few feet of her physical body, although she was unable to see it herself. To be classified as a genuine crisis apparition, however, the phantom should have been witnessed not more than twelve hours before or following the "creating incident" - the crisis which caused the phantom.[14]

Haunting Apparitions

This description relates to the hundreds of much-publicised cases where an identical figure of an apparition is observed on several occasions in the same place, but not necessarily at the same time, by various witnesses. Naturally, this mainly refers to phantoms of deceased people or animals, but it has been known to include crisis apparitions as well as those of the living.

The cause of haunting apparitions appears to be the same as that of all such phenomena, namely that someone at some time has created an intense thought-picture of himself or his pet animal in a particular situation at a

---

[14] Owen, Dale (1863) *Footfalls on the Boundary of Another World*. London. Trubner & Co; Gurney, E. Myers, F. and Podmore, F. (1886) *Phantasms of the Living* Vol II 'Further Visual Cases' .

specific site. The image is created by the mind linked with brain, as in a dream, and is transmitted unconsciously. It is well known that it is possible to record "brain waves" on an electro-encephalograph, and it can be seen that when the subject is dreaming (which can be ascertained by observing "REM" or rapid eye movement), the waves are very active, sometimes more so than when a subject is awake.

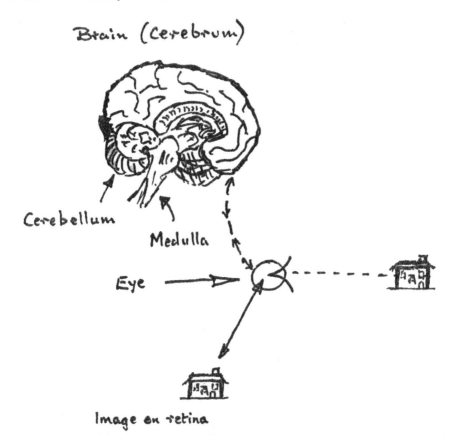

Fig. 6a - NORMAL VISION OF PHYSICAL OBJECT

During times of stress, such as physical pain or emotional upset, the waves are extremely active, and it is believed that when they reach a certain pitch a telepathic image is being transmitted. A subject standing on the site to which the image is being transmitted would, if a telepathic recipient, probably see the image (see figs 6a and 6b). The telepathically created picture, or telepathic hallucination, can exist for months, or even years in the locality, and will therefore "outlive" the agent.

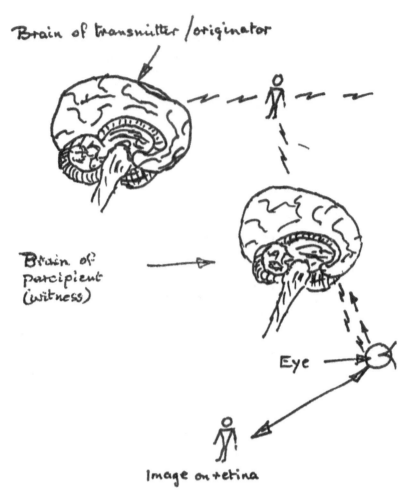

Brain of transmitter /originator

Brain of
parcipient
(witness)

Eye

Image on retina

Fig. 6b - VISION OF APPARITION

This provides an answer to the problems of ghosts walking through walls or closed doors, for both encumbrances will have been erected or constructed since the image was created. If a ghost is haunting the ground floor of an old house, which is then demolished and a block of offices erected on the site, the ghost will not necessarily disappear, but will merely continue to haunt the spot which, as a result of the development, might have become a typing pool or even a ladies' lavatory.

Whether the ghost continues to be seen or not depends on the time the image was created in the first place. If it were transmitted at, say, eight o'clock in the evening, there is little likelihood of it being witnessed and it will therefore "die". On the other hand if the image first appeared at ten in the morning, then provided the area involved is often visited the ghost will continue to be seen, possibly appearing through a partition wall (fig. 7).

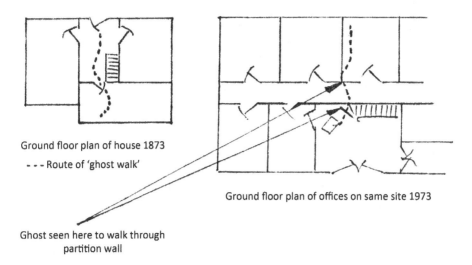

Ground floor plan of house 1873

- - - Route of 'ghost walk'

Ground floor plan of offices on same site 1973

Ghost seen here to walk through
partition wall

Fig. 7 - THE HAUNTING OF A NEW BUILDING CONSTRUCTED ON THE SITE OF
AN OLDER BUILDING

In the retina of the human eye there are about 100 million light-sensitive cells capable of transmitting an impression to the brain, although there are only about a million nerve fibres leading back to the brain. And not all the cells need to be stimulated for an image to be transmitted. It should be remembered that the sensitivity of the eye is less pronounced at night because only the "rods" which do not register colour, are functioning. Whereas each "cone", the part of the eye which notes colours, is connected to an individual nerve fibre, a cluster of rods is needed per fibre. Thus sensitivity of vision is reduced, since whatever a number of rods "see" can only be transmitted via a limited number of fibres. But what about the working of this operation in reverse?

It is known that memory is carried in the form of a closed circuit, an electrical impulse travelling round a loop of cells in the brain, and these electrical charges, travelling constantly round a brain-cell, are renewed by the sodium potassium process.

A small electrical charge given to the nervous tissue of the brain where both sight and hearing are recorded can make a subject "see" flashes of light, or "hear" bells ringing or "knocking sounds". It is also possible to make a subject cry out, though he will usually report that it does not feel like some external force causing the action, but rather resembles "an inward compulsion". It can thus be seen that an upsurge of electricity at a receptive point of the mind area can cause phantom images. Since the 1970s some researchers have considered electrical stimulation of the temporal lobes of the brain as offering clues to the nature of paranormal experiences.[15]

Whether or not the reader accepts this theory of ghosts is, of course up to him/her, but remember that electromagnetic waves are in the atmosphere all the time. Some of these are converted into a visual image such as that on a television set, and others to sounds that radio receivers can pick up.

As far as is known, the foregoing explanation for hauntings covers all, or practically all, aspects. Not only can mental pictures of people be transmitted but also those of animals, coaches and cars, as well as mental noises. The latter are heard as human voices and are often linked with the appearance of an apparition.

In terms of the processing of mental images, it was proposed by one leading 20th century researcher G. N. M. Tyrrell that there were two stages in an apparitional experience. In the first stage, the percipient unconsciously experiences the apparition, and in the second stage the unconscious information is then processed into consciousness, through dreams and certain waking experiences that resemble ordinary cognition and perception.[16]

But I have found no evidence of any genuine cases where actual conversations have been carried out with the ghost, for the phantom voice which has been created at a different point in time to that in which the witness finds himself. It may have been two weeks ago or even 200 years ago, although the reader may find it difficult to accept the possibility of such phenomena continuing over a lengthy period.

We now come to another indication of a haunting – a reduction in temperature. Radio waves are affected by heat and other differences in atmospheric pressure, and it seems that fairly frequently, either just before

---

[15] Persinger Michael. (1979) 'ELF field mediation in spontaneous psi events.' In Tart, C. T., Puthoff, H. E. and Targ, R. (eds) *Mind at Large*, 191-204. New York: Praeger; Persinger, Michael. (1985) Geophysical variables and human behaviour. *Perceptual and Motor Skills* 61, 320-322.

[16] Tyrrell, G.N.M (1953) *Apparitions*.UK. Duckworth

the appearance of an apparition or for the duration of the phenomena, the surrounding temperature drops appreciably.

This phenomenon cannot fully be explained, but it may be that two telepathic waves linking together create a fluctuation in the temperature, extracting energy in the form of heat to produce an image. Because of this a close watch on a thermometer during telepathy experiments could be valuable.

The continuation of a haunting over a very long period, say 250 years, can be explained by regeneration. This is associated with the drop in temperature. It would appear that for a mentally created image or phantom to be witnessed over a period, re-energising by heat extracted from the atmosphere and the individual is necessary. If this is not done, by means of the image being seen, then the phantom will gradually fade away. In some instances this can be seen to occur in stages.

During the 18th century a ghost of a woman in red shoes, a red gown and a black head-dress was observed in a little-visited corridor of a mansion. Many years passed before the apparition was seen again, and by then, perhaps because the original full description of the ghost was not then known, it appeared as a female in a pink dress, pink shoes and grey head-dress. She was not witnessed again until the mid-19th century, when the figure had dwindled down to "a lady in a white gown and with grey hair". Just before the Second World War all that was reported was "the sound of a woman walking along the corridor and the swish of her dress". In 1971, shortly before the demolition of the property involved, workmen "felt a presence in one of the old corridors". In another case in Scotland an apparition originally reported as dressed in green seemed to have faded to a yellow by 1905 and was reported in the 1970s as wearing a dress the colour of ripe corn.[17]

There are many other cases, however, where the apparition is still seen as clearly today as it was when first witnessed, because of repeated viewings. One of the classical cases is as Hampton Court Palace, where the ghost of Catherine Howard has been seen so many times by the occupants of the "grace and favour" flats that the description is hardly ever likely to change.

To illustrate the overall theory it will perhaps be helpful to quote two examples of known hauntings.

---

[17] Green, Andrew (1976) *Phantom Ladies*. UK. David and Charles Ltd.

An elderly executive of a nationally known company was devoted, as was his wife, to their pet dog. They had no children. One day the animal suddenly died, to the extreme distress of the owners, who were sufficiently distraught to need to take a couple of days off work in order to recover from the shock. For months afterwards the man would sit disconsolate, gazing at a particular spot in the garden where to quote his own words, "he could still see the poor old dog in his favourite corner". After a time, and having purchased another dog, the couple recovered, but the "picture" had been created. Over a year after the death of the original pet a neighbour reported that he had seen the ghost of the animal sitting in a corner of the garden.[18]

Another case involves two better-established ghosts. In a public park in Surrey female moans are sometimes heard issuing from a particular mound in the side of a sand-hill. The site is believed to be where a pregnant nun was buried alive by her murderer, the monk who was to become the father of the child. Assuming this story to be true it is easy to imagine the feelings of terror with which the man committed the deed; near insanity as he was, the strangulated moans of his victim were impressed on his sub-conscious mind. So distraught was the murderer that he decided to drown himself in a nearby pond. It is not difficult to imagine him "seeing himself" walking round the lake, plucking up sufficient courage to jump. The two ghosts, one auditory and the other visual have both been experienced in recent years.

Some phenomena, such as doors opening and the apparition being seen in a mirror, are all part of the telepathic hallucination. The doors do not physically open and the ghost is not actually reflected visibly as a physical object. Some years ago sceptics asked how ghosts could wear phantom clothes: the answer is obvious. The clothes form part of the "picture". There cannot be many people who would find themselves in a situation where the mind created a naked image. As far as I know there are no naked ghosts, although owing to the popularity of the permissive society I should imagine that there might well be some in a few year's time.

Mediums

In case the reader feels that he should learn more about mediums, I should explain that these people are more acceptably termed "sensitives"; some are genuinely clairvoyant and/or clairaudient. They are not necessarily

---

[18] Andrew Green had personal experience of seeing the apparition of a dog in the house of an uncle at Sidmouth in 1951. Enquiries revealed that the form resembled the beloved pet of the previous owners.

aligned to any particular religious faith. It is believed that such talents or qualities as they possess are latent in many people, and can be developed.

The reader may be interested to learn that, according to *The Mediums' Book* by Allan Kardec, translated from French in 1876 by Anna Blackwell, at that time over 40 differing types of mediums were classified. Some of these may today sound a little ambiguous, such as the "Motor mediums" who "produce the movements of inert bodies. These also were very common"; but on the other hand "mediums for musical effects: these obtain the playing of certain instruments without human contact" were "very rare". "Rare" also were the "Pneumatograpraphic mediums" who produce "direct writing". Both "Polyglot" and "Illiterate" mediums were also "very rare".

Anyone attending a séance with a medium should certainly adopt an open mind, for an antagonistic attitude will become obvious to the sensitive and will genuinely affect results. Offence to the individual concerned, and consequent ill-feeling can also result.

Because of the powers of sensitives it may be advisable to know the address of one who lives locally. They can prove valuable as a source of information and helpful in some cases of hauntings. It is my understanding that because their minds are super-sensitive to telepathy and unconscious telepathy they are able to receive mentally phrases and comments made at some time in the past, in the same way that witnesses mentally receive images created earlier. Thus a medium can "hear" the voice of a deceased person, and will impart her knowledge of what it said to the related sitter at a séance.

I believe that the process is as follows. When someone was in a particular frame of mind, and thinking intensely of the sitter, who may be a friend or a near relative, the thought was "concentrated" enough to become a permanent fixture in the atmosphere. It does not matter whether the originator of the thought is dead or alive, and the medium is able to receive the thought through having a sympathetic individual with her. The sympathy, or catalyst, lies in the fact that the sitter is, or was related to or associated with the creator of the thought.

I have unfortunately caused much embarrassment during a couple of sittings by thinking with great intensity of a close friend and a particular phrase he used. On both occasions the mediums present gave me a message from my "departed" companion which of course, was the phrase I was thinking of. The person I was concentrating on was, and I hope is still, very much alive.

There is a rather similar case of ESP recorded in the SPR *Proceedings* XXXV and referred to in the Presidential Address in 1972 by Professor C.W.K Mundle, MA when a new "entity" came through. The voice and mannerisms of speech of this entity were identical to those of a boy whom the sitter, Dr Soal, had known at school twenty years earlier, and whom he thought to have been killed in the War. Three years after the meeting with the medium Dr Soal discovered that the 'communicator' in question was still alive.[19]

I am not denying, however, that there do appear to be some genuine cases of seeing the future.

Phantom voices on tapes

A lot of publicity has been given in recent years to the phenomenon of "Raudive voices" recorded on ordinary tape. Named after their discoverer, Dr Konstantin Raudive of Germany, these voices are claimed to be those of deceased entities speaking mostly in German, and can be heard on playing back a recording of a normal session of, say a radio broadcast, or even a general conversation or interview.

Considerable investigation is being carried out all over Europe on these claims, and much controversy is raging as to whether they are truly paranormal, caused by psychokinesis, telepathy, auto-suggestion or perhaps some other means. Tests are becoming more sophisticated, employing such apparatus as "Psychofons", Faraday cages (an enclosure screening the microphone from extraneous transmissions such as radio broadcasts), high impedance voltmeters, oscilloscopes and low noise amplifiers, and the recording of transmissions on ultra-short waves (3m.100 MHz).

The problem of interpretation of the extra voice remains. I would recommend that anyone interested in pursuing experiments on this form of phenomena should be directed to the extensive literature on the topic since that of the Paraphysical Laboratory at Downtown, Wiltshire, who published numerous reports on the work being carried out and the work of David Ellis at Cambridge in the 1970s; international studies have also been commenced in the decades since.[20]

---

[19] Mundle, C.W.K.(1972) 'Strange Facts in search of a theory'. Presidential Address. *Proceedings of the Society for Psychical Research*. Vol 56 Part 207 January 1973.

[20] Ellis, David (1978) *The Mediumship of the Tape Recorder*; UK.D.J. Ellis; Parsons, Steve & Cooper, Callum A. (2015) *Paranormal Acoustics*. UK. White Crow Books.

But before spending a lot of time and money in constructing what could be very expensive equipment, it should be remembered that magnetic tape recorders can easily act as radio receivers, and have been known to pick up local telephone conversations.

One recording in Britain of "ghost voices or noises" was effected at Bircham Newton in 1972, and this was broadcast several times by the British Broadcasting Corporation, mainly by Jack de Manio in an early morning radio programme.[21]

Although it might be worthwhile to take up this branch of parapsychology, how one can achieve any proof as to the paranormality of the sounds received constitutes a major problem; the origins of such recordings must also be investigated to eliminate deliberate or accidental deception and naturally occurring sounds.

One example of a pitfall that the keen and over-zealous amateur can experience was a tape-recording, believed to be of "Raudive voices", which turned out to be not a recording of a German-speaking entity but a backward recording of an English broadcast. The accident was caused by the playing in error, a four-track tape on a two-track recorder.

Physical Mediumship

This subject has been touched on earlier, and in any case does not really relate to genuine ghosts. It is merely the doubtful production of physical phenomena by doubtful means. Admittedly in some cases physical entities or parts of entities, such as hands, feet or faces, appears to have been manufactured by ectoplasm emanating from a medium in trance. Alternatively, psychokinesis is produced, raps are heard and objects moved.

Poltergeists

This phenomenon, one of the most publicized and so often misunderstood, is comparatively easy to establish in most cases as nothing more than psychokinesis (sometimes referred to as telekinesis), though exactly how this operates is not yet fully known. The fact that certain people can cause objects to move simply by willing them to do so must now be accepted. An increasing number of pseudo-scientific explanations are being offered, but none as yet that the scientific world in general is prepared to accept.

---

[21] Green, Andrew (1973) *Our Haunted Kingdom*. Wolfe Publishing.

Since many of the popular cases of "ghosts" are, in fact, nothing but incidents of poltergeist activity, it would be wise to attempt to understand the basic phenomena.

Primarily, what happens is that objects are moved by an unseen force. Vases, mirrors, chairs, tables, books and clothes are thrown about or moved from one spot to another. In some instances loud crashes and other inexplicable noises are heard, peculiar odours waft about, and occasionally "whispers and murmurings" are included in the phenomena. In many poltergeist cases a child at the age of puberty is involved and appears to be the "modus operandi". Sex certainly seems to be the root cause of many incidents of PK (psychokinesis). A fairly common poltergeist phenomenon involves bedclothes being moved or thrown about, and this seems to occur more frequently when an elderly person is the "agent". Subconscious sexual frustration may be a cause of this.

One American investigator found that the object-throwing sessions in a couple of cases went in cycles which corresponded to the menstrual cycles of young adolescents living in the affected property. Some mediums, especially physical mediums, have been known to enjoy a sexual climax during the creation of phenomena, and the number of female mediums who have passed through the menopause and are perhaps suffering from frustration is significantly high. There are very few genuine mediums who are mothers and even fewer with more than one child.

When it is realised that the highest concentration of electrical energy in the human body is at the age of puberty and just before a menstrual period, it is perhaps not difficult to appreciate that it is at these times that unconscious thought is also at the peak of its power.

There are numerous reports of poltergeist activity abruptly ceasing, or fading away, when the youngsters concerned "break through" into adulthood. The adolescent herself may be completely unaware of the fact that she is responsible for the chaos and will strongly and emphatically deny it. Others may embellish the phenomena. A careful watch during periods of activity may indicate that the girl or boy in questions appears to be either sleepy and lethargic, or just the reverse, high spirited and giving the impression of being "high". These periods of uncharacteristic behaviour will stop within seconds of the poltergeist activity ceasing, and the "agent" will regain normality.

If the human mind is strong enough to create a mental picture in another person's mind, then surely there is no logical reason for supposing that it is of insufficient power to move objects. Some people believe that psychokinesis is a sub-layer of consciousness, which (as any hypnotist will tell you) exists on various levels.

In 1952, with six colleagues, I decided that it might be interesting to see whether it was possible to smash an ordinary glass tumbler by "thought power". We all concentrated on exploding the glass, and after 14 ½ minutes the glass shattered. This cannot of course be classified as evidence of PK, for coincidence and high-frequency radio waves cannot be ruled out as a possible cause, but all seven of us were mentally exhausted after the experiment. None of the group were nearer the glass than two feet six inches. One experiment in association with PK is to protect an object which it is intended to move by means of an infra-red beam falling on a photo-electric cell. One such trial indicated a relationship in rhythm between the breathing rate of a physical medium present during the experiment and the movement of the assigned object.

As stated in the Preface, other new scientific studies into the subject have been carried out especially, it seems in Russia and America. In Russia, Alla Vinogradova, in the presence of several witnesses and whilst being filmed, was able to move an object weighing 10 grammes and "make an aluminium tube rotate". She was questioned as to her subjective feeling and replied that she experienced no stress during the sessions but felt that the energy came from her solar plexus (the question of sex again?) and confirmed that what is gradually becoming accepted, namely that anyone can train himself to become adept at psychokinesis. It has been possible for this young Russian to move round objects of some 200 grammes weight by "thought"; for more detail I would refer the reader to the *Journal of Paraphysics.*[22]

One area where success has been achieved is recording rapping and knocking sounds attributed to poltergeist activity. Such sounds may potentially encompass a wide range of reported noises, including "thumps, rappings, scraping, ticking noises, self-playing instruments and physiologically impossible vocal utterances" but following suggestions that such sounds should be subject to acoustic analysis, most interesting results have been obtained. In 2010 research by Dr Barrie Colvin revealed that

---

[22] *Journal of Paraphysics* Issued by the Paraphysical Society, Downton, Wiltshire. Vol. 6. No. 2, 1972.

instrumental analysis of the wave form arising with raps attributed to poltergeists showed a distinctive pattern differing from sounds produced in the normal way. Whereas with normally produced raps the acoustic pattern began with a sharp spike in sound which then declined, those attributed to poltergeist raps began relatively quietly then built up to an intensity, suggesting that the sound was created within matter it appeared to emanate from (for example a wall or the headboard of a bed). Examining a range of samples on different recording media obtained between 1960-2000, the effect is only identifiable by way of instrumental analysis by subjecting such sounds to acoustic analysis. If this pattern can be found elsewhere and cannot be explained, this suggests the existence of a repeatable effect, and collecting such samples should be the aim of all researchers into poltergeist effects.[23] One of my own experiences with a poltergeist subject was a result of being called upon by the *News Chronicle* in 1956 to investigate Shirley Hitchings "The Poltergeist Girl of Battersea". The girl in question, a fifteen-year-old, was a typical agent.

She was able to cause knocks and raps to be heard and felt anywhere in the room, and claimed to communicate with "the entity" involved by this means. It was noticed that every time she was asked if the poltergeist would knock on a specific spot she would close her eyes briefly, as if concentrating her thoughts, and refuse to sit down with both legs off the floor. Before the possibility of PK was admitted, it was believed that the raps could have been caused by her "cracking her bones". The phenomena were attributed to a "ghost" affectionately termed "Donald", claimed to be Louis Capet, illegitimate son of Louis XVI of France, from the 18th century. The case was characterised by extensive production of writing attributed to the entity which was spread over many years; I received three letters and a Christmas card from "Donald". Further details on this with a reproduction of one of the letters, will be found in *This Haunted Kingdom* (1973). Manifestations persisted for years afterwards and the subsequent lengthy history is covered in the book *The Poltergeist Prince* (2013) by James Clark and Shirley Hitchings.[24]

---

[23] Crabbe, John (2002) 'Some Paracoustical Proposals' Journal of the Society for Psychical Research Vol 66 No. 868; Colvin, Barrie(2010) 'The Acoustic Properties of Unexplained Rapping Sounds' in the *Journal of the Society for Psychical Research* Vol 73.2 Number 899 pp 65-93.

[24] Andrew Green took the view that "the girl had written the letters; it may have been that she had written the material whilst in a semi-trance and had only vague memories of the incident. I had made no mention of receiving the correspondence when I met her, but she

Rapping phenomena have a long history, as with a case observed in 1877 by the physicist Sir William Barrett, in 1877. When the girl agent was lying on a bed he found that the "geist" would provide the same number of raps as a figure *he himself thought of*. Poltergeists in general are thus seen to be associated with specific individuals, and seldom with buildings, sites or objects. Further evidence for this conclusion comes from a director of a Midland manufacturing company which suffered from this type of phenomena for some 15 months. "It was only when Miss "X" left our company that the disturbances ceased," he told me. The director of a chain of tobacconists, referring to similar incidents in a retail shop in the South-West, said, "I am quite convinced that the trouble emanates from one of the girl assistants. When she leaves it will stop". And so it turned out.[25]

Mixed hauntings and poltergeist cases

In some cases the phenomena appear to be a mixture of both a haunting and poltergeist activity, with physical manifestations being reported over a lengthy period at particular premises despite changes in occupiers. A good example is the Seven Stars Pub at Robertsbridge in Sussex near the home of the author, which saw changes of licensees a dozen times in 32 years between 1971-2003, with all of the 12 licensees, their families and their staff reporting poltergeist-like activity. Such cases may reflect the pressures arising from the pub trade and the stresses imposed on domestic relationships (the pub had a history of unhappy and broken marriages finishing in divorce).

An extensive computer study of characteristics in some 500 historic poltergeist cases conducted in 1979 revealed that whilst 75% of poltergeists seemed to be of short duration and focused on a single individual, around 25% might last more than a year and seemed place-centred, enduring like a traditional haunting.[26]

---

specifically asked whether I had heard from 'Donald'". However, subsequent evidence and research and Shirley's own account casts doubt upon her having any responsibility for the correspondence which was far more extensive than Andrew Green ever learned. See *The Poltergeist Prince* (2013) by James Clark and Shirley Hitchings.UK. History Press.

[25] Barrett, William (1911) 'Poltergeists Old and New' *Proceedings* of the SPR Vol 25 377-412; Air Heating case, Yorkshire in Green, Andrew (1973) *Our Haunted Kingdom*. USA. Wolfe Publications.

[26] Gauld, Alan and Cornell, Tony (1979) *Poltergeists*. UK. Routledge Kegan & Paul.

In some cases, the fear triggered by the experience of an apparition (real or imagined) may trigger poltergeist activity created by the emotional reaction of members of the family concerned, but the existence of such a pattern may indicate a more complex relationship between the individuals and the environment. Such cases illustrate the need to consider both the psychology and personal circumstances of the witness and also wider environmental factors, including the history of the site.

Seances

Too often treated as a Christmas game or a party pastime, the holding of a séance should really be taken much more seriously, especially as many people regard such gatherings as meetings for the purpose of conversing with the dead.

Ghost-hunters at some time are bound to hear of séances, be invited to one, or feel that they may wish to attend such a function, and therefore a few words concerning these meetings will not go amiss.

The most popular method is for a group of people (not thirteen in number) to sit round a polished table with their hands lying flat, face down on the surface. The sitters' fingers touch those of their neighbours, and each person's thumbs also touch each other, to create a circle. Another method is to sit with the hands palms uppermost, for some believe that this position will both generate and receive power. The lights in the room should be dimmed and smoking forbidden during the session.

Seances arranged by religious groups usually commence with the singing of hymns, and a crucifix is sometimes prominently displayed. The significance of these precautions has been described as "ensuring that evil entities are not contacted."

For the safety of the individuals concerned (the "sitters") it is desirable to omit all persons of nervous disposition, those endowed with vivid imagination, and, as stated earlier people who are argumentative or antagonistic.

The method of establishing communication, if no known medium is present, is to wait a few minutes in silence and hope that something will happen – the table move or rock, or raps be heard. It is desirable, if any result is to be obtained, for all the participants to try and think of nothing, keeping their minds blank. This may be difficult, and the recommended method is to think of a blank cinema screen or a white sheet.

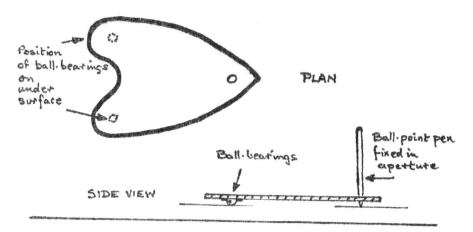

Position of ball-bearings on under surface

PLAN

Ball-point pen fixed in aperture

Ball-bearings

SIDE VIEW

'DETECTOR' MODEL
(Prototype designed by author)

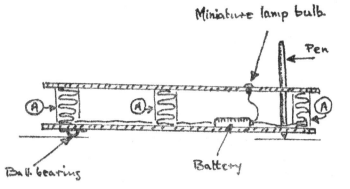

Miniature lamp bulb

Pen

Ball bearing

Battery

(A) — Three springs connected with flex to the battery which operates lamp when 'top deck' is pushed. Springs encased in metal foil.

Fig. 8 - PLANCHETTE

A previously elected "spokesman" will, at intervals, enquire "is anyone there?" which may be "answered" by a movement from the table. The spokesman should then suggest an agreed code of "one knock for "No", two knocks for "Yes"'. The movements of the table may well be accompanied by knocks or raps apparently emanating from the table itself. Once "contact" is made, the spokesman has only to ask those questions that have been agreed or are suggested by the other sitters, but – as can readily be imagined – real information is limited if the only answers possible are an affirmative or a negative.

Another less sophisticated type of séance involves the use of an upturned wineglass: the index fingers of all sitters are placed lightly on the top (the actual base of the glass). Letters of the alphabet, written on pieces of paper or card, are placed all round the edge of the table; the word "Yes" is placed at one end. The hope is that the glass will, after a few minutes, begin to move of its own volition, and questions can then be directed at it in order to establish the identity of the entity and anything else one wishes to know.

I would warn the amateur that for the first few minutes the sitters are likely to accuse each other of pushing the glass. Sometimes the culprit is very obvious. At other times, it will be impossible to tell which of the group is responsible, and more often than not, in any case, the "pusher" will not recognise his involuntary action.

So popular has this game become that Ouija boards, the sophisticated way of using this system, are now produced commercially. They consist of a large board around which the letters of the alphabet and the words "yes" and "no" are placed. A large pointer on a pivot is fixed in the centre, and when the sitters' fingers are placed lightly on top of this the pointer will start to spin and move the letters.

Yet another form of "communication with those who have passed on" is by means of the planchette (fig.8). Here again the index fingers of the sitters are placed lightly on the wooden top to create "the power", and the unit will "write messages" on paper supplied beneath, or so it is hoped. This is sometimes referred to as "automatic writing", although this term properly refers to cases in which only one individual uses the planchette.

It is almost unheard of, in my opinion, for any of these "expeditions into the unknown" to provide any proof or evidence of "life hereafter". Much nonsensical information will be provided, most if not all of which will be found later to have originated from one or two members present. The movement of the table is more often than not caused by psychokinesis, though sometimes by a sitter's knee.

If a sensitive is present at the gathering, the sitters are expected to turn the palms of their hands towards him, in order to direct and concentrate the power in the direction of the sensitive.

How does one know whether one is so sensitive? One answer given has been that at such sessions "one begins to feel light-headed and starts to dream." This reply was given by a woman who eventually became a genuine trance and clairvoyant medium.

One experiment would be to ask all the sitters to clear their minds and think of nothing during a session; the ghost-hunter can then concentrate on one or two words which have been previously written down. It is surprising how often it will be found that these words will be written by the planchette or spelt out by the Ouija. Does this constitute further evidence of telepathy?

I would certainly not recommend ghost-hunters to spend too much time participating in séances. I would suggest that anyone who really wishes to pursue this particular course of investigation should attend a séance organised by a local group, after first studying the very useful little pamphlets *Hints on Sitting with Mediums* and *Trance Mediumship,* both published by the Society for Psychical Research.[27]

---

[27] Society for Psychical Research 1965, available from the SPR library, London.

CHAPTER 4

Equipment and its use

Basically the essential needs for an efficient ghost-hunter are an adaptable, enquiring – even inquisitive – open mind, a general liking for and understanding of people, a sense of humour and a strong desire to achieve a satisfactory conclusion to an undertaking. This calls for a lot of patience. A good memory for what may appear to be useless information also helps, as does an enthusiastic outlook. This description may give the impression that the qualities needed are those of a good detective, and this is true, for that really is what ghost-hunting is all about; attempting to sort out the genuine from the fraudulent, the accurate from the imaginative.

As far as equipment and apparatus are concerned this will obviously depend on the funds available, the intensity with which the investigator wishes to pursue his interest, and which particular branch of the subject he intends to investigate.

For plain ghost-hunting various pieces of equipment have been mentioned in earlier chapters, although some may appear a little too sophisticated to start with. In fact the only really essential "tools of the trade" are a shorthand notebook, a ball-point pen and a measuring tape. It should be emphasised that instrumental evidence is only part of a wider picture which must be built up in an investigation. Unfortunately, too many individuals and groups believe that obtaining any sort of image or recording is sufficient and tantamount to proof. Yet at the same time they fail to provide anything about the circumstances and context in which the image or data is obtained. Unfortunately, merely securing unusual readings or images of one kind or another does not establish anything as proof unless the recordings or readings can be put into a proper context, along with all other factors which need to weighed and considered as evidence.

But before setting out on a hunt it is advisable to have a digital camera or camera fitted for flash operation and at least two films. A simple camera is quite adequate, except that not all of these are fitted with time exposure controls, which may be found necessary. A vital accessory for camera work is a tripod. Another suggestion is to take a polaroid instant-print camera, for the type of photograph produced by this can be extremely useful in certain circumstances.

Video and film cameras can be extremely useful for ghost-hunting and monitoring premises, especially in cases of poltergeist activity.

Tape and digital audio recorders are recommended for use during interviews, provided the subject agrees and is not too conscious of being recorded; they are also important, when investigating a haunted building, for recording any noises which are heard. When interviewing the appearance of a recording device is sometimes inclined to inhibit the witness's freedom of speech, especially among witnesses, who may be embarrassed or afraid of being recorded. Remember that there are still quite a few people who dislike being photographed, let alone being presented with inanimate object into which they are required to speak. If using a tape or digital audio recorder for interviewing, try to make it as inconspicuous as possible by putting it on a table and ignoring it. Remember also a lot of people, particularly older people, do not want to be involved with social media and you should not casually publish statements or personal details in any form of social network or via the internet without clear permission to do so.

If making written notes, make sure you collect and write them up as soon as possible after the interview as inevitably the passage of time will mean you are likely to forget crucial details. The closer the note is made to the time of the interview the more accurate and reliable it is likely to be as a record of what was said.

A thermometer is also a very useful piece of equipment; digital models are widely available. However, what is important is not so much the type of equipment but the capacity to use it in a scientific manner and according to agreed international standards for scientific measurements. (See Appendix two). The location of the measuring instrument too must be documented; it is not very helpful to simply say "The temperature of the stairs was 21°C at 10pm". Whereabouts on the stairs was the temperature information obtained? Was it at stair level or somewhere above stair height? What type of thermometer was used and how long was the measuring period? It can take several minutes for a thermometer to stabilise and be able to make a reliable temperature measurement. Regard should be given to the information supplied by the manufacturer but this is frequently ignored by users.

It might be a good idea to make up a "kit-bag" in which all the apparatus is stored is stored for use at a moment's notice; and some ingenious and enterprising companies now manufacture ghost hunting kits. Bearing in mind that the ghost-hunter is a "specialist detective", a good quality magnifying glass is another article that must be included.

As well as the notebook, graph-paper will be required for drawing the necessary plans of property, sites and specific areas. Several pieces of coloured chalk will also be found helpful for marking objects or sites of articles likely to be moved.

The inexperienced investigator may be surprised to learn that he should include in his kit-bag a supply of thin nylon thread and black cotton, a quantity of flour, graphite powder and a small paint brush. But remember that you must be determined to identify normal causes of phenomena in cases which initially appear to involve the paranormal. It is for this reason that your attitude and the methods you adopt must be those of an open-minded private investigator.

The black cotton and nylon thread are used for the detection of physical agents moving objects and opening doors or windows – either accidentally or intentionally creating fraudulent phenomena. Flour is used to detect human footprints and handprints, and the brush and powder to heighten finger prints.

If there is a possibility of night work, and there should be, then a good quality torch, with a couple of candles and some matches, will obviously be necessary. It might be a good idea, if you feel that there is a likelihood of some hours being spent on the property or site, to equip yourself with camping gear, complete with thermos flasks.

Another essential is an Ordnance Survey map of the area, as well as a 2 ½ inch-to-the-mile map. It is the information from these that may provide a possible answer for the phenomena. The use of maps in ghost-hunting is dealt with in more detail in a later chapter.

Ghost-hunting is one of those activities which is liable to call for inventiveness where equipment is concerned, especially as ever more and more sophisticated equipment becomes available.

Infra-red filming equipment and thermal imaging devices are a valuable addition to anyone's equipment, as well as night vision goggles, but these may require some expertise in interpreting the pictures. It is desirable to attach the flash to a motion detector so that when anyone in a room moves the equipment will be triggered.

Photo-electric cells, also wired to the flash camera, are useful for the dedicated investigator, and so is a geological map of the area, for this reveals natural faults in the strata of the subsoil. A voltmeter for checking electrical power faults, in cases where lights "go off and on", is another helpful accessory to the ghost-hunter's equipment. Since the 1990s Electromagnetic Frequency Meters have often be used but these are of questionable use unless you know how to operate them. Basic EMF meters provide only amplitude information and without frequency information it is almost impossible to determine source of any field.

During the 1970s and 1980s a combined detecting unit devised by leading members of the Society for Psychical Research, Tony Cornell and Alan Gauld was deployed. It consisted of a camera linked to a tape recorder, linked to a photo-electric cells, linked to a noise and vibration detector, a small electric bulb, a sensitive wire circuit and a buzzer. The idea was that if anything made a noise in a room which had been wired and sealed then the camera would automatically take a photograph; a drop in temperature of more than a certain number of degrees would also cause the camera to operate. In both cases, of course, the tape-recorder would also be switched on and light and buzzer would operate.

Incorporated into the prototype was a draught-detector which, when the vanes were turned, would also operate the equipment. But the problem was to decide on how sensitive the pieces of equipment should be. If it was too sensitive, someone sneezing in the next room, for example, would cause all the equipment to operate: the light would come on, the buzzer sound, the camera would flash and the tape recorder would start.

This illustrates the problem of the sort of equipment required to detect everything that is likely to happen in a haunted room and yet allow for normal incidents of everyday life. A large lorry driving past the property created sufficient vibration for the unit to operate; but of course one cannot hope to exclude all such outside interference.

Unfortunately, although deployed at approximately 100 locations over some twenty years, the device was seldom activated and little of any note was recorded.[28] One can only attempt to modify and adapt. What may be quite suitable for detecting phenomena in a country mansion, miles from the nearest property, would probably be utterly useless in a tiny room in a terraced house in the centre of London.

---

[28] Cornell, Tony (2003) *Investigating the Paranormal*. Helix Press. New York.

It must also be remembered that a phenomenon can never be relied upon to "perform", and seldom follows a regular pattern, despite assurances by witnesses. Be prepared, therefore, for spending perhaps an hour on wiring up and sealing off an affected room, and waiting in a cold dark corridor surrounded by switches and wires, only to find that the phenomenon, if it starts at all, suddenly commences in another room on another floor of the building. Such occurrences can cause irritation, amusement or suspicion – the latter especially if there is a youngster around at the time.

An empty house is of course ideal, particularly if there is a team of investigators, for then each person can be responsible for a specific area, and the team can make certain that every incident is recorded or noted.

To complete your "tool-bag" you should include a spring balance and a strain gauge, both of which can be used to record the weight of objects which have been moved and perhaps the strength needed to close a door.

A couple of hand mirrors for the detection of fraudulent activity, a spirit level and a compass are accessories that may also be called for in certain cases, as well as string, plumb line and impact adhesive. This last item is used to stick the "detecting cotton" across apertures such as fireplaces, windows and doorways. And don't forget that in some ancient manor houses secret cupboards, priests' holes and the occasional tunnel are still in existence and must be noted and examined.

The examination may yield some interesting information for the owner of the property. It was discovered in one case that the entrance to a secret tunnel had been blocked up with a very heavy wardrobe and over the passing of years the existence of the passage had been forgotten. The complaint was that "weird noises, raps and knocks" were heard to come from the cupboard and were accompanied by a "cold blast of air", yet the owners of the affected house were reluctant to move the unit. Finally, they were persuaded that to complete the investigation it was vital to move the wardrobe. When this was done the entrance to a stairway was revealed. It was unfortunately necessary to disturb some of the panelling surrounding the formerly concealed doorway, but this was offset by the delight of the owners at discovering a secret passageway.

The stairs led down through the wall to an old ivy-covered window which had long been forgotten, it was established that the noises were caused by birds nesting in the ivy and tapping with their beaks against the hidden glass, the sound travelling up through the passageway, which acted as a sounding chamber. The cold draught was caused by wind coming through the old keyhole.

Common sense is also a vital quality for the good ghost-hunter. In the early 1950s a team of investigators, including myself, were called upon to "get rid of a ghost" in a small private hotel in London. On arrival, I was told that there were, in fact, three ghosts that haunted the establishment. The most important was the phantom of "a little green man" who had several times been seen walking down the stairway, while the others were "just weird bumps in a bedroom" and "clattering in the kitchen".

On asking if it would be possible to interview the latest witnesses of the little green man I was informed that the couple were away on holiday. So all we were left with was the bumps and clatters.

The question of bumps in the bedroom was dismissed in a matter of minutes, for it was obvious that the weird noises were caused by wind coming through an airbrick in the wall facing the prevailing wind, travelling through the cavity wall and, on reaching a small and badly fitted built-in cupboard, causing the doors to rattle. On duplicating the noise of the "ghost" by lightly pushing the loosely fitting doors, I was told that the ghost must be in there with me. The proprietress of the hotel was out on the landing being too scared to come in at the time, but when I explained the trouble and demonstrated the cause of the haunting she appeared to be disappointed.

The "clattering over the kitchen ceiling" was also caused by the wind, which was blowing small stones from the pebble-dashed outer wall down to the corrugated iron roof of the kitchen porch. The owner of the hotel seemed even more disappointed at this discovery. When we discussed arrangements for a return visit to question the witnesses of the little green man the lady, a little shame-faced, admitted that the couple involved "were rather imaginative and very fond of the drink".

I should like here to digress for a moment to point out just how far some people will go to obtain publicity – and also the need to be prepared for the unexpected. The owner of this particular hotel was obviously reluctant to let the investigating team depart and suggested that we should hold a séance. In order to placate her (after all, we had "killed off" two of her ghosts) and to test out the medium who had joined us just for this case, we agreed.

The medium went into a trance and pronounced "there is buried treasure in the wall. I can see a pile of coins in a hole in the wall. The hotel owner was absolutely delighted and said that she "had always hoped to find some buried treasure". She then insisted that we knock a hole in the wall at the point indicated by the medium while in trance.

Having borrowed a couple of heavy hammers and a cold chisel (other tools for the "bag"), two of us proceeded to comply with the request. I must admit that when the top layer of paper and plaster had been removed and a large circular piece of plaster was revealed I was a little apprehensive. Unfortunately for the treasure-seekers, this was merely where a plumber had finished off concealing the water pies leading to a radiator fitted in the hall on the other side of the party wall.

The owner, left with a gaping hole in her sitting room wall, appeared only slightly disappointed and requested that we should then hold another séance. Ever anxious to please our "client", the medium went into a trance again and stated that the treasure was not in the wall at all, but under the floor!

One hour and six floorboards later a tunnel was revealed beneath the building. According to a chalk notice on one of the walls this had been constructed in 1810. It was some 150 feet long and led to a summer-house at the bottom of the garden.

Without taking up the floor boards from several other rooms we were unable to ascertain where the "official" entrance should have been, but presumably there was a trapdoor somewhere to make access a little easier. The only object that was fund in the tunnel was a dead mouse. We declined the suggestion that we should dig up the floor of the tunnel.

The proprietress finally admitted that she had hoped would authenticate at least one of her ghosts so that she could obtain some publicity, and she had already told the local paper of our planned visit. She was quite pleased, nevertheless that we had discovered a secret tunnel. Unfortunately, the local press were not impressed and the whole exercise proved fruitless as far as publicity was concerned. The whole building was pulled down in 1970 and a block of flats erected on the site.

Never assume that because the first call has been welcomed the following visits will meet with the same attitude. The people involved may well have become bored with the incidents, found they had perfectly rational explanations, had the ghost exorcised, or even have developed a fear of the phenomena to the extent of believing, as some do, "that interference will only anger it". But, because of the unpredictable nature of the phenomena and the fact that incidents cannot be guaranteed to occur at specific times, it will probably be necessary to arrange several visits the site. It is therefore advisable at the outset to make it obvious that you may very well need to come back, possibly several times. Never give the impression that the case is not worth bothering about (even where this is obviously so), for your reputation may be affected and it may be difficult to find another interesting case.

Initial contact with a witness should be made preferably by telephone or personal contact. Although it would be courteous to confirm your call by letters or e-mails, requests for information or an appointment by post hardly ever seem to be answered. Your approach should be friendly and informal, for this will encourage witnesses to talk freely and, at the time, to adopt a more relaxed attitude towards the phenomena.

Uninhabited Property

Naturally, before carrying out an investigation in empty premises, it would be necessary to obtain full permission from the owners, who may be the local Council, or a private individual. Establishing the address of the owner can be irksome, but this information can usually be obtained from either the local Rating Office of the Council or sometimes, the Police.

Once permission to carry out an investigation on the property has been received I would recommend that you keep the letter as proof, and take it with you when carrying out your investigations. One good reason for joining a Society or forming one yourself is that officials are likely to look with greater favour upon requests from a group, or a member of a recognised body, than from an unknown individual.

It is in the empty building that one can really carry out an unhindered investigation, using all the equipment to the full (except perhaps in cases where local and national journalists are involved). Remember, however, that the Press and media can be of considerable assistance in providing past histories of properties, can often help in locating previous owners and are also sometimes the first to hear of a ghost. The attention of the Press will usually prove to be a mixed blessing; it provides publicity for the work you are doing, but also attracts interest from cranks.

Inhabited public property (pubs, stately homes, etc.)

Licensees and proprietors of public houses and, to a certain extent, owners of historic houses, are usually quite accommodating when it comes to a quiet interview for a couple of hours, but tend to be less enthusiastic if a full scale investigation is requested.

This attitude could suggest the authenticity of the phenomena is suspect; for what better way to authenticate a haunting that to report to the Press that the case has been investigated by a parapsychologist? And merely to provide uncheckable information, such as "one of our visitors saw a ghost a few months ago", or "the barman was frightened at the apparition he saw on New Year's Eve in the cellar, but he has left now and I don't know where he is", cannot be considered as evidence of any real value.

Obviously the more publicity given to a property open to the public, the more attractive it will be to visitors, and it is therefore often worthwhile for owners to provide information about their "ghost, however imaginative or fraudulent the phenomena may be. Since the mid-1990s it has become common for owners of alleged haunted premises to cash-in on the reputations of their properties, and this may provide an incentive to exaggerate or invent experiences, if any, associated with the site. Whilst in principle the owner of premises is entitled to charge a fee for hire of premises you should be careful of any situation where such a clear commercial incentive exists and of groups that offer 'haunted evenings' or 'fright nights' to the public in return for often substantial fees. Regrettably such stunts have become increasingly common in recent decades, leading to a number of events being routinely televised on commercial channels. Almost invariably such events are devoid of any serious and scientific content, entirely lacking in any controls or rational assessment of evidence, and operate as a branch of the entertainment industry (under which heading they are often classified by broadcasters). The possibility that events may be staged for a commercial motive, as with the plethora of examples of fake spiritualist mediums dating back to the 19th century needs to be considered. Certainly, the lurid and sensational claims for phenomena will at once be recognised by any intelligent viewer as arising in circumstances that are either highly suspect or so lacking in proper controls that they should be disregarded as evidence of anything – except perhaps gullibility.

There are some people who would even offer more money for a haunted house that is for sale, just for the interest and "thrill" of "owning" a ghost. Unfortunately, the Trades Descriptions Act has not yet been applied to such a claim, but there have been several instances of people purchasing "haunted" property only to find the ghost, if ever it existed, had not been experienced for many years. The reverse is true as well, but mainly in council houses, and the cases are generally those of poltergeist activity.

When dealing with property open to the public it would be wise, during the initial discussion, to explain exactly what you hope to achieve, and to obtain approval for bringing in the equipment at some convenient time. Ascertain at the time same time the location and availability of power-points and the position of the fuse-boxes.

In the past luminous paint could prove of use in order to locate small items "in flight" during poltergeist activity or séance conditions, and in addition to illuminate people suspected of being the cause of the phenomena. The method to adopt is to attach pieces of card coated with the paint to their sleeves or cuffs, shoes, trousers or skirt hems; but never paint the skin with luminous material, as it is slightly radioactive and may cause a rash on sensitive skins. Motion sensors and infra-red beams provide a better alternative for the 21st century.

Ideal equipment, once sophisticated and expensive, would be closed circuit television. Cameras and transmitting sets with digital recording apparatus can often be affordable and are now a staple in the equipment box of most ghost hunting groups.

Other detecting equipment can be as simple as sand, or, better still, sugar. Human feet on either of these substances will not only provide visual evidence but also scrunching sounds, if shoes are worn (or perhaps startled exclamations if the walker is bare foot!), and will warn the investigator that a physical intruder is afoot.

One of the advantages of being a member of a local research society is that equipment, which should be pooled for the benefit of the group as a whole, can be borrowed by individuals. Also the inventive members and those in specialist fields can often produce suitable apparatus at a fraction of the cost that manufacturers would charge. There are not many companies who would be prepared to make single items of specialist equipment in any case.

Equipment for automatically recording such phenomena as table movements during séances has already been constructed, and it is not difficult for the imaginative individual to adapt and improvise on other readily available apparatus. If you have a clear idea of what you are trying to discover and record, it is comparatively easy to create the necessary instruments.

The production of a case full of apparatus at the commencement of an investigation in itself constitutes a test, for the witness of genuine phenomena will be, or should be, impressed with the serious nature of the ghost-hunter, while the fraudulent will be worried by the prospect of being exposed. They may well start to modify their statements to such an extent that the value of pursuing the case may become doubtful.

Also be prepared for equipment to break down. A problem that often seems to affect certain investigators is the failure or malfunctioning of equipment at a haunted location, often at a crucial moment. Many researchers have a suspicion that this may happen more frequently than might reasonably be expected by chance at haunted locations, and some even recognise it as a form of phenomena in its own right. However, you should be careful of jumping to conclusions. What may seem like a mysterious failure in a reputedly haunted location during the night might have no such connotation in a mundane location like a busy shopping centre during broad daylight. Is it an effect caused by the operator or by something in the environment? A frequently encountered cause of apparent equipment failure is actually operator inexperience, when ghost hunters fail to properly familiarise themselves with the operation of the equipment beforehand. Whatever the case, equipment may fail, batteries may be drained of power, or cameras cease to function at crucial moments and a malfunctioning device may compromise readings and any conclusions you draw from them. It is best to be prepared for such eventualities so far as is possible by having spares or back-up equipment. Whatever the case if such events occur you should make sure they are recorded like any other incident.

These are just some of the hazards of ghost-hunting, I am afraid.

CHAPTER 5

Site examination

Not necessarily before interviewing the witness or witnesses, but at some time during the investigation, it is essential fully to examine and survey the site of the haunting in relation to the basic information obtained. By this I do not mean merely looking at the house or whatever the affected property is and mentally describing it as "old" or "new".

In order to produce a thorough and comprehensive report which makes full allowance for natural causes of phenomena, a full knowledge of the area is required. Basically an Ordnance Survey map will provide considerable information but, as stated previously, a 2½ inch map offers much more information, for it shows wells, houses, footpaths and other natural features in much greater detail and clarity. It even indicates the shape of buildings.

A geological map is also useful, as this will provide details of the natural strata of the subsoil, information which will be valuable in assessing the cause of phenomena, especially where movement is concerned. A basic knowledge of geology will also assist your work generally. Advanced techniques for examining beneath the ground are available in archaeology.[29]

For example, on the south coast of Dorset only a few inches below the topsoil lies several feet of greensand, oolite, and then lias or slate. This is constantly moving towards the sea because of the numerous underground springs which carry it, like a solid tide, to the beach and the cliffs. The result is here that numerous buildings are forever cracking, "groaning" and shifting, but as far as I know there are only a couple of ghosts in the centre of this particular locality, at Lyme Regis.

In 1908 a spontaneous fire on the cliff top at nearby Charmouth, which was known as the Lyme Volcano, was believed to have been caused by the friction of the iron pyrites in the combustible layer of slate; but some gullible and imaginative folk, without even examining the site claimed that the weird flames were those of a witch who was burnt there in the 17th century, Incidentally, there was no proof of that either, but there was proof of paraffin being used to keep this tourist attraction alight!

---

[29] Clark, Anthony (2004) *Seeing Beneath the Soil: Prospecting Methods in Archaeology*. UK. Taylor Francis.

ANDREW GREEN

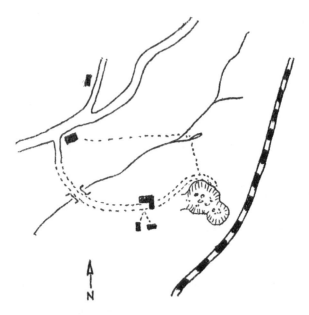

Gravel pit - 30ft East
Stream - 35ft West
Railway - 75ft East
House on steeply inclined gravel overlooking pit.

Note: Noises heard only on East side about 'Xmas time'

Possible causes

1. Frost affecting pit workings
2. Subsidence of gravel subsoil following rain/frost
3. Vibration from passing trains
4. Stream beneath property?

Fig. 9 - SKETCH PLAN FROM ORDNANCE SURVEY MAP TO INDICATE
POSSIBLE CAUSES OF PHENOMENA

In fig. 9 a sketch plan of an area taken from an O.S. map is accompanied by border notes concerning possible factors which may well account for the phenomena in the affected property. It is sometimes helpful, in order to gain a visual and more accurate picture of the landscape, to sectionalize an area and extend contour lines to give a side view of the locality. This illustrated in fig. 10. Simply copy the original contour lines on to a piece of paper, draw sufficient horizontal lines to cater for the number of contours involved and then join the two by means of vertical lines, at the spot you wish to sectionalize. Obviously, computer mapping techniques can also be used.

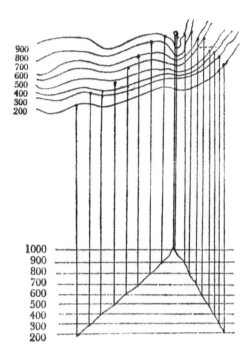

Fig. 10 - SECTIONALISED LANDSCAPE DRAWN FROM ORDNANCE SURVEY MAP

Closed mines and quarry workings are another source of "phantom" noises such as moans and groans, for wind whistles though the old tunnels, whose acoustic properties are inclined to increase the intensity of sound. The constant pressure on old and neglected roof trusses is also likely to create ghostly sounds, and so too is subsidence of nearby property. Long-forgotten tunnels and caves create problems not just for motorway constructors but also for ghost-hunters puzzled by what may appear to be poltergeist activity. Here again subsidence will eventually prove to be the cause.

If the property is on clay or chalk, heavy rain following a drought may well cause inexplicable noises such as creaks, knocks and groans. Subsoil of sand or gravel can cause some movement of objects under similar circumstances.

Your aim should be not to dismiss the haunting by providing *probable* causes, but to examine every possible natural feature in order to understand the phenomena more fully.

It is surprising how often mist is mistaken for the phantom of a "figure in white", especially in woods. The natural phenomenon of mist in small clouds may not be appreciated at the time of seeing what appears to be a ghostly apparition drifting along a few inches above the ground. It is also surprising how often a column of smoke with a long triangular shape is seen as a human figure. On obtaining information as to the exact location of the incident and the time of day and year, you should visit the site and ascertain whether the ground is low-lying, swampy or marshy, and the proximity of ponds, lakes and streams. Remember also that campers and gypsies may frequent the site, and that there is a possibility of bonfires and steam from cooking pots. Every eventuality has to be considered. Was the incident in the morning, when mist rises from the damp ground, or at dusk, when the dew is falling?

One incident puzzled a couple of amateur sleuths in the late 1960s. Several campers in a small clearing in a wood had frequently and regularly heard what they described as "a sort of whistling moan", which they attributed to "a ghost". It was found that some yards away a small dip in the ground was partially filled with household and some industrial rubbish. A few feet further on the ground fell away to a treeless valley. Although a few of the braver ones had carried out a rough search for the phantom, they had been unsuccessful, though they had learnt of some weird stories from local residents.

When a ghost hunter with a more professional approach arrived he first checked the time at which the sounds were heard, and established the wind strength and its prevailing direction from a local meteorological office. A few minutes later, after examining the pile of junk, he was able to explain the "ghost" was merely the wind blowing up the valley into the pit, through a couple of old metal cylinders which acted like organ-pipes. When the cylinders were twisted to face across the wind, the weird moanings ceased.

This incident may remind readers of my emphasis on the need for common sense and logic, together with a sense of humour, when dealing with reports of hauntings. The story had already been reported to the local press who had published it under the heading "Campers find ghost in local wood". No mention was ever made of the death of the ghost. It was not newsworthy.

Strange lights at night are more often than not due to marsh gas, or car or train headlamps. Sometimes ball lightning can account for weird effects, and this is probably the origin of the "burning ball of light" that has been seen in rural areas in the autumn and winter. One of these has even become renowned as a warning of disaster for a particular Irish family in the South. Reflections in windows, greenhouses, cold frames and on pieces of shining metal also account for some of the reports of "flashes of light".

Incidentally, the age of window-glass, despite common belief, can be ascertained by measuring the top of a pane and then the bottom. There may be as much as 2mms. difference, for over many years gravity will cause the seemingly solid material to "flow" downwards and thus be thicker at the bottom. The relevance of this is that the flow is not even, and imperfections already in the glass, which have become accepted by the house owner, will alter imperceptibly, changing the view of the light at a certain angle. The witness not realising this, may claim that a light seen as a normal occurrence up to then has become a "ghostly" one.

One example of this movement of glass in connection with phenomena occurred at Caterham. A particular window set at an angle beside a fireplace in a 17th century house had peculiar marks resembling a hand-print in the centre of the pane. The legend connected with this peculiarity was that an old woman looking through the window one day had seen her son attacked and murdered, and to steady herself from the shock of this tragic experience had put her hand on the glass, creating an indelible mark on the pane. Exactly how this was created is a mystery, but at least two witnesses told me that they had seen the marks on the glass, and that they were perfect reproductions of a smallish palm print. Years later when I enquired about the possibility of photographing the window, I was assured that the print had "mysteriously faded away".

This is a good example of a story being created to account for a physical phenomenon. No doubt when the glass was originally made and still pliable some youngster had accidentally put his hand on it and got badly burnt, unconsciously creating the basis for an attractively romantic myth (although in all fairness there is in this case a thin possibility of the murder story being true).

On examining a specific building it is advisable to find out exactly how old it is and what materials were used in its construction: the value of this information lies in the fact that various items used in buildings are affected in different ways by certain weather conditions, and could thus prove to be the cause of problem noises and movements.

The age of a building can usually be found in the deeds of the property or in maps of the area; owners, in this respect, are usually fairly accurate. Tenants, however, not being really interested may be vague, so contact should first be made with the owner of the building. Details of some historic buildings are available from council offices, where such buildings are graded into various types for preservation purposes.

Timber-framed houses are more liable to stresses than the conventional type made of brick or stone. Remember that the ancient method of wooden framing is now regaining popularity, and several estates of contemporary style property in fact consist of timber-framed houses. Damp, woodworm, death-watch beetles, rats, mice, and birds in particular have all been found to be the cause of "ghostly noises" in this type of house, whether it be old or new (Woodworm only affects houses in certain areas, usually those built on chalk). Specific areas in which to look for "outside agents" are skirting boards, floor-boards, lofts, airing cupboards, lean-tos, and faults in cavity walls.

The belief that old houses are more frequently haunted than new ones may well be due to the greater number of natural noises in older property. In fact the number of reports of phenomena in new property is higher than that relating to older premises. Ignoring the obvious possibilities, the noises may be caused by crumbling plaster, or very likely by expansion and contracting of the ancient timbers – particularly if central heating has been installed. The unaccustomed warmth not only causes floor boards to creak but also furniture to groan, and these noises frequently become more intense at night when the heating circuit is off.

Another aspect of modern phenomena is pools of water on the floor, and the number of cases in which this occurs is on the increase. The culprit is more likely to be the central heating system than the pet cat or dog. In a well-sealed house without double insulation, the internal warmth causes a lot of condensation, with the result that the owners find unaccountable patches of dampness or puddles of water in certain rooms. Since these are usually in rooms with closed windows, witnesses are puzzled. "It didn't rain so there couldn't be any leaks in the roof ", or, if it did pour, "the windows were all closed. I can't understand it", are two comments from people who have reported such phenomena. The water may be in the centre of the room, for the edges being nearer the warmer walls or radiators, will have dried out. Also, of course, the floor may be uneven, especially in ancient property.

One of the causes of "phantom footsteps", I believe, is the regular contraction of floorboards, starting from the wall nearest the heat from a fireplace, a night storage unit, or a radiator. Once one board contracts and creaks, it releases pressure on the adjoining board which then also contracts and creaks. The process and sound travels across the floor at such regular intervals that "footsteps" are very often thought to have been heard.

Isolated natural incidents can quite easily create ghost stories. One night when I was in a hotel bedroom on the point of going to sleep, I was aroused by a sudden but regular tapping which stopped after a couple of seconds. A few minutes later the sound was repeated. Because the hotel was set deep in the countryside, I thought at first that the sound was caused by a bird tapping at the window. After the fourth repetition I opened the window and heard a couple of bats twittering in the eaves above my head. But this was not the cause of the tapping. I finally gave up the search for the disturbance and went to sleep.

In the morning I enquired as to the reason for the noises, my host looked embarrassed and pleaded ignorance of the cause of my disturbed night. Further enquiries from members of staff extracted a story that "a nun was bricked up in a room a couple of hundred years ago and occasionally one hears her tapping to get out of her living tomb".

Unfortunately for the story teller, I found the reason for the irregular series of taps, and it was absolutely nothing to do with the nun. In a cupboard above the hand basin was a jug half filled with water. Over its edge a face-cloth dangled in the liquid, acting as a pump. The water dripped silently on to the shelf, but when the pool on the wood was large enough it overflowed into the basin beneath with a regular tapping sound.

The chambermaid who "didn't believe in ghosts any way" was delighted when I demonstrated the cause of the "ghost tappings", for she had always been mystified for some time as to why the jug was nearly always empty in the mornings even when there had been no guests in the room. She thought someone had drunk the water. One wonders how many visitors to the hotel were convinced that they heard the poor nun trying to break out to freedom.

It must be realized that some people, because they genuinely *want* to experience phenomena, will both conjure up and adapt incidents to prove that they have, despite the fact that in some instances the evidence is nothing out of the ordinary when examined dispassionately.

One example of this happened in 1973, when a plumber told me with some excitement that he had been in a haunted house and had experienced a ghostly phenomenon. The reason for his belief was that, having turned off the main water supply to the premises, he returned to the kitchen only to find water still coming from one of the taps. "There was no-one else in the house" he assured me, "it was really weird". I suggested that water will take a few moments to drain away from a closed-off system and he seemed quite disappointed, but admitted reluctantly that this was possible.

Details of another minor incident may provide further evidence of a purely natural occurrence which could easily have been taken as a paranormal phenomenon by someone wanting to experience a ghost. While working in my garage during the autumn I was disturbed by bumps suddenly occurring on the roof of the building. As in the case of the dripping face-cloth, there was a series of regular noises, and it was some minutes before I realized that apples were falling from an overhanging tree and bouncing on to the corrugated roof.

Recalling the haunted hotel and my exploits in knocking a hole through a partition wall, the ghost hunter will obviously note any new structural changes such as the installation of radiators inside the haunted building. The noises of central heating systems, especially at night, can be really disturbing. Bangs from empty rooms, creaking floor boards from deserted corridors, mysterious whisperings and hummings, even human-like howls, can all be associated with this modern facility. Remember this when noting the details of the phenomena.

The natural element of wind can cause a new country-dweller or a newly-moved city family some concern, nearly always at night, when traffic sounds are at their lowest level and the area is hushed or silent. As well as moving tree branches against windows, wind will howl in chimneys (particularly if they are fitted with cowls), whisper through shrubs and tall grass, and whistle round television aerials. Noises caused by the vibration of objects on outer walls of houses will often be carried inside and may be described as made by "unseen entities". In every case you should seek to determine when precisely the witness or witnesses (if it is a family) moved into the property and assess whether lack of familiarity and the novel stimuli of a new environment may have been playing a part in generating unusual experiences. It may be noted that many incidents reported as being of a ghostly nature begin on the night that a family move in or very soon afterwards. This may arise from misperception or it could be an aspect of paranormal experience where a combination of a specific place and a particular individual are responsible for triggering phenomena.

Another effect of wind and air-pressure is the opening of doors, a very common symptom of a haunting. One young waitress in the South even claims the "ghost" opens the door for her! The sudden movement of one door may easily cause another to open or partially open. If the handle is loose or only partially engaged it may well move hours later due to some local vibration such as a nearby footstep. Anyone facing the door at the time might understandably assume that invisible agents were at work.

I advised earlier that the materials of which the affected property has been constructed should be identified, and it is understandable that readers should consider old timbered properties more likely to be haunted than others. But what may not be realised is that many ancient houses in England incorporate sandstone; in the South-East this is known as Hastings sandstone, and it has a peculiar trait.

This rock, conspicuous in the ruins of Hastings Castle, is in layers or strata, one or several of which ironstone, which has the property of conducting voices like a telephone. This phenomenon is often demonstrated by the official guide at the castle, who takes groups of tourists to visit the dungeons carved out of the solid rock. After requesting silence, the guide takes one of the visitors to a cell and asks him to whisper a message. The other visitors are able to hear the words in spite of being many feet away from the whisperer.

Is it therefore so unusual to hear noises which originate in a house built with this stone within its walls? Naturally, the rock does not have to be Hastings sandstone to produce this phenomenon. All that is necessary is a material which contains a band of ironstone or iron pyrites in it.

It would be interesting to find out whether thin sheets of lead conduct noises in the same way as ironstone, for such material can still be found in old buildings, on roofs, window ledges and, in certain cases, as damp courses. Tin will certainly act this way, and I have found instances where this cheap metal has been used to patch damp spots in outer walls.

Moonlight can produce weird lighting effects, especially when clouds are present, and on one clear night I was myself mistaken for a genuine ghost. The incident does illustrate how easy it is for the imaginative to scare themselves.

The occasion was a visit of mine to the site of the famous Borley Rectory, the "Most Haunted House in England", and the incident took place in the road beside the long-neglected garden. Together with a young colleague I was patrolling the area during a scientific investigation in August 1952. The time was 1.45 in the morning, and we were walking down the hill from the original coach house.

To clarify the circumstances it is necessary to describe our clothing. My associate was wearing a black balaclava helmet, a pair of very dark khaki trousers and a light "desert issue" Army jacket and light fawn trousers. Although August, it was very cold, and my jacket was just slung over my shoulders, my chest and arms being covered with a heavy knitted pullover, and my hands pushed deep into my trouser pockets.

On hearing a cyclist approaching from behind, we moved into the ditch and waited for him to pass, gazing idly over the moonlit fields opposite the site of the Rectory. As the cyclist heard us he uttered a piercing and hair-raising scream. We turned, and saw the rider pedalling furiously down the hill as if pursued by the Devil himself. It was only when, puzzled we looked at each other that we realized what the witness must have thought. One legless headless torso next to a bodiless head and an unconnected pair of trousers!

The cyclist apparently felt it necessary to take a second look at the weird manifestation, and turned round at the bottom of the hill to cycle back up the hill. As he approached I flapped the sleeves of my jacket, and he screamed again and turned rapidly into the nearby coach-house driveway.

We were a little puzzled later to learn, when we asked the owner of the house about the possible identity of the night-rider, that there was no-one in the village who had any cause to ride a bicycle at that time of night and there was no cyclist in the household. We learnt that the gentleman in question, James Turner, was intending to write his own book about his experiences at Borley. Although this appeared in 1970 as *Sometimes into England* published by Cassell, little coverage is given to the haunting and certainly no mention is made of the mysterious cyclist.

So, during moonlight nights, beware of people dressed in unconventional attire, especially since some teenagers are keen on such garb, including black cloaks and wide-brimmed hats. Seeing a figure in such an outfit could easily create a report of a "ghost of a highwayman".

Fishermen often pursue their sport late into the evening and ideal clothing for sitting on river banks or beside fish ponds, especially at night, is the modern version of the duffle coat complete with a hood. There are more than a few occasions upon which a silent hooded figure standing on a bridge in the moonlight or sitting hunched up beside a stream has been mistaken for a monk, so it is a good idea to check with local fishing clubs before following up such tales.

If a haunted house is a genuine Elizabethan or Tudor property there is always a chance that there is a priest's hole or some secret cupboard incorporated into the structure. The location or even the existence of all these hiding places may not be known to the occupiers, and this is a good reason for making an accurate plan of the building showing dimensions both inside and out. Should the owner explain usually with pride, that "the walls are three feet thick", or some other impressive measurement, remember that this is wide enough to provide a small cell or hidden cupboard.

It has been known for a younger member of the household to hide in one of these with no intention of causing trouble, but the result is the same – "weird scufflings, scratchings" and similar "paranormal phenomena" are heard. A few years ago one of these cupboards was discovered in a "haunted" smuggler's house in Sussex and contained considerable evidence that it had been used by children – perhaps during a hide-and-seek session – and also by mice, for many years. Once it was cleaned out no further phenomenal noises were reported.

Even builders of Victorian and more modern buildings have been known to construct a hiding place or secret cupboard in the walls, and the number of tunnels that still exist, leading from the main house to some other part of the property, such a summer-house is quite considerable.

One amusing incident which took place in 1971 provides food for thought in connection with cases where noises in the loft are reported. A family of four had moved into a terraced house in London, and noticed that their neighbours complained about the sound of "rats in the attic", and said that they were informing the Council.

A few days later a loud crash, accompanied by several bumps, was heard coming from the new residents' attic. They were scared, and asked the Council to investigate, mentioning at the same time "the rats are next door". With the usual speed of official bodies the Council representative called three weeks later, by which time more unearthly noises had been heard. "Bodies being dragged across the floor", "weird scrambling noises and shuffles", "whispering", were but a few of the descriptions given by the nervous tenants. The Council official clambered into the loft, and surprised exclamations were heard by the family grouped on the landing below. Then silence. Minutes passed and there was still silence. The family grew apprehensive until footsteps were heard, and the official returned with a grin on his face. The explanation was that immigrants, realising that few people in the road ever used their loft space, had decided to offer extra accommodation to their friends. This was accomplished by knocking holes in three party walls below the roof, carefully dodging the chimneys and putting in camp beds over the joists of neighbours' bedroom ceilings.

This scheme had been successful in three houses and they were now at work on the fourth, but the noise made by the lodgers had caused their activities to be discovered. Extra accommodation for fifteen people had been supplied, albeit temporarily, by this method, and at least one local family had been scared by their unknown "ghostly" boarders.

In cases of poltergeist activity, and also in some others, reports are often made of "cold spots" in specific areas, such as landings, bedrooms or even in a corner of a field. They are often explained away by stories of murders or suicides. Many remain a mystery, as does the bedroom in the Crown Inn at Oxted, Surrey. This is one of the coldest rooms I have ever visited and apart, from the alleged haunting by "Aggie", there appears to be no explanation for the freezing atmosphere. The landlord has kept a fire alight in the room for ten days in an attempt to improve the temperature, but without success.

Do not dismiss these "cold spots" out of hand, but look first for a logical explanation. Many cases will be found to be caused by wells or underground streams rising near the surface of the soil.

Short of digging up the affected spot, the problem is how to discover a stream hidden perhaps by several feet of earth or inches of concrete.

The simpler methods are to search through old maps of the area, enquire from the local Council, or even talk to an elderly local inhabitant. Another method is to employ a water-diviner or to use a hazel twig yourself; it seems that divining is now becoming "respectable" and officially recognised. I am not suggesting that everyone can become a dowser, but with a modern apparatus this faculty is certainly easier to develop, and several helpful publications are available on the subject.

Pendulums have been used to locate objects for many years and many explanations have been offered as to how they work. An affinity existing between the operator's mind and the object to be found seems likely, for numerous successful demonstrations have been given showing that it is possible to use the same pendulum to find iron, water, coins, and even missing people, merely by thinking of them while holding the thread and waiting for the weight to gyrate over the location, either on the site or over a map of the area.

I have tried out one modern version of the pendulum, the Omni-Detector Kit, to locate a missing well in my own garden merely by holding it over a rough hand-drawn sketch plan of the site when over 50 miles away, but so far attempts to find coins or the well have proved fruitless. I am convinced, however, that some people do locate such treasures by this method.

Some claim that it is this form of divining which has been developed into the "science" of radiethesia, and ouija boards can also be used in the detection and cure of diseases. But divining does not really have anything to do with ghost-hunting, although it can be regarded as an aspect of parapsychology. Claims that spirits can be contacted via dowsing equipment remain unproven and in almost all cases movements of a rod or pendulum can be attributed to the operator (albeit unconsciously in many cases) or other natural causes.[30]

Since the advent of double-gazing, especially the "do-it-yourself" kits, the number of reports of moans and groans in the night has slightly increased. This weird effect is merely the wind whistling through the gaps left by badly fitted internal frames. In the majority of cases the culprit is the handyman who has skimped on the job in an attempt to save money, has completed the project badly, or alternatively has used the wrong quality polythene, which is always subject to stress and strain and can seldom be guaranteed to give a complete seal.

While we are on the subject of construction, remember that dozens of reports of hauntings are made every year in new properties. Usually the authenticity of such cases can be dismissed after only a few minutes spent interviewing the witnesses. It would seem that modern standards of building leave a lot to be desired.

In one block of flats in Surrey, completed in August 1971, it was found necessary to replace *every* door within eight months of completion. Many had swollen to such an extent that they could not be opened, others had shrunk and repeatedly opened of their own accord, "most mysteriously", and some had split and cracked. The reason for this was of course that the timber had not been properly dried, and central heating had such a bad effect on the wood that there was nothing to be done but fit new doors. Unfortunately the need to replace the surrounding frames was not realised,

[30] Maltby, Prof. cited in Nichols, Beverley (1966) *Powers That Be*. UK. St Martin's Press. Fraser, John (2013) *Ghost Hunting: A Survivor's Guide*. UK. History Press. Murdie, Alan (2012) Ghostwatch column *Fortean Times* No.279. January 2012.

so that now, as far as new tenants are concerned, doors still stick and "open on their own".

There are occasionally reports of spontaneous outbreaks of fire in some poltergeist cases. One of the most famous, or perhaps infamous incidents in Sussex was investigated by a researcher during 1970/71. He attributed the events to an "evil influence but one which was kindly disposed to children". The reason for this qualification was that the flames, which he had watched start inexplicably in one room, consumed the wallpaper and paint from the window-frame and surrounding down to floor level, but failed to destroy a child's toy and a bag of sweets on the wooden sill. The long curtains were burnt but only up to the window level, and the floor was untouched.

Apart from fraud, obvious causes and childish pranks, there seems to be no logical or scientific explanation for such outbreaks, which are fortunately rare. The obvious causes are faulty electrical wiring which has sparked off some easily combustible material, or magnification of the heat of the sun by a flower vase or even an aquarium. Less obvious causes are fumes from paraffin or oil-heaters and even leaking gas, especially the North Sea variety. Household flour and sawdust are equally inflammable under certain conditions. Mice and rats can also cause fires by chewing away the insulation fabric away from electrical flex, for nest building, thus causing short circuits. These creatures can also create the sounds of "phantom music" when gnawing the felt pads from piano wires, or in one case, those of a harpsichord. They have also proved to be the cause of "mysterious bell ringing", by running along the wires which operate the bells.

Any ghost hunter who has solved a haunting by detecting a natural cause may become familiar with the impact that fear can have eroding the well-being and happiness of the residents. Fear and anxiety may cause psychological illness and worry which is the background to the poltergeist. What may be important is not that there is any reality in the particular ghost or haunting, but rather the strong effect that suggestion plays on the minds of the inhabitants. The feeling that the group is prey to an outside force may help generate the phenomena by adding to the stress on members, both individually and collectively.

Site examination also involves obtaining the necessary archaeological information, and this is dealt with in the following chapter.

CHAPTER 6

Early history of the area

An important part of any investigation of a haunting is recording information about the former and original buildings on the site, for some aspect of these may well have some bearing on the phenomena being examined. Maps and early documents are obvious sources of information, and a visit to the local museum or contact with the archaeological society of the district will probably provide basic knowledge of the site and its earlier constructions. Originals or copies of illustrations of the property should be obtained if at all possible. It would be ideal to have photographs of the building at each stage of its development, but of course this is seldom possible.

The history of a haunted building or buildings can be highly significant. As will be seen on referring to fig. 7 in Chapter 3, what may have been haunting a house in say the 19th century, could well continue to "inhabit" the site for several decades, despite constructional alterations, demolitions and developments.

Owing to the constant demand for new houses, councils and developers are always searching for suitable land on which to build. Not only are numerous old houses being demolished to make way for blocks of flats or completely new estates, but age-old rubbish pits and even former graveyards are being taken over as suitable for development. I am not suggesting that burial grounds are haunted, but many people seem to associate them with ghosts, ignoring the fact that very few people have been known to die in graveyards or to have been closely linked with graves (apart from grave-diggers). But because the association does exist in people's minds, quite normal occurrences on the site, or in the new buildings constructed on it, are often assumed to be paranormal phenomena.

So strong is the feeling that ghosts are associated with the dead that in Hampshire a builder was convinced he had seen a phantom, because he had disturbed an old grave-stone which was being used in the path of a public house undergoing modernization. The fact that the grave-stone had been brought from the churchyard half a mile away about fifty years earlier seemed to have no effect on this conviction.

While we are on the subject of tombs, I was rather amused by the story in this connection concerning a family in Guildford. A man had cleared a churchyard in Abinger in 1968, and removed two lorry-loads of broken tomb-stones to construct a path in his own garden near Guildford some miles away. This was done quite effectively, but in 1970 the owners of the property, although delighted with the general appearance of the path, were worried by the fact that the previous owner had laid the stones face uppermost so that the fragments could be read.

So disturbed were they that they took them all up, reversed them and laid the stones face down. At the same time one stone, which was complete, was deliberately broken into fragments because "no one would walk on it" and the younger member of the household "had felt a presence whenever she was near the stone". It would have been interesting to blindfold her and guide her down the path to see if she could locate it "blind".

The general attitude seemed incredible to me, for the stone in question had never been used: it was merely a spare waiting for a "customer". This provides a good illustration of the power that imagination can sometimes have. Future archaeologists may well be puzzled by finding what appears to be a 19th century graveyard in an area marked on the map as "flood fields", and which has been the back gardens of property since 1961. Bones will never be found, for the soil is far to acid.

While ascertaining details of earlier buildings on a site it is also advisable, if possible, to find out the uses to which they were put. One of the most publicized cases in 1971 was in Norfolk, where a building constructed as a hangar on a war-time aerodrome has been converted into a squash court. Not only were unusual noises and voices, associated with the maintenance of aircraft, tape-recorded inside the building, but a figure RAF uniform had been seen on several occasions. This particular case appears to be one of the genuine ones that have developed in over the years since the end of the Second World War.

Another similar history is that of Manchester Airport, where staff of a freight-forwarding company have witnessed the phantom of an RAF pilot walk through a partition wall in the evenings. The building was originally an administrative block of offices constructed for the Air Force in the early days of the war. Even a couple of the Airport Police admitted that they had seen the figure.

Open ground is perhaps more difficult to check on, for obviously thousands of incidents could have occurred there which could account for a current haunting. In these cases the local police and / or newspaper may be able to assist. This type of enquiry also relates to areas on which a building has been constructed for the first time; even though all sources of information may give no indication of previous property, archaeological and historical experts may well produce some satisfactory answers.

Where there has been constant re-building on a specific site, compiling a complete historical record of each occupation could obviously involve long and perhaps unrewarding research, especially as you can never be quite sure which piece of specific information or detail you are searching for. Each particular period of occupation and each specific use could well account for the origins of a haunting. Long-established domestic use could suggest a well-established family or household, any member of which may easily have become so attached to the building or part of it that a ghost has been created.

If there is an indication of shop premises having been on the site, it can be valuable to find out what sort of business was carried out. Perhaps it was a coffin-maker or a funeral director? At the same time you must try to establish what deaths have occurred on the site, how, why, and when. Was there a murder there, was there perhaps a suicide, a fight or an accident? Although violent, sudden, or unexpected deaths do not necessarily create ghosts, many cases of hauntings do seem to be associated with such incidents. You cannot be expected to compile a complete dossier from the year 1066, but the more information you can obtain the better.

It is hardly sufficient to learn that "someone died there in the 18th century" for this tells you so little as to be virtually useless. It is essential to find out who died, how and why and exactly when, and then attempt to obtain documentary proof. If there were two or more people involved, for example in a murder case, it is of course desirable to investigate both in your searches. Be prepared to discover that studying ancient documents can sometimes be tedious, for old church records are often rather lax, and in certain parts of the country common surnames abound.

If there was some form of religious building on the site such as a temple, a convent or an abbey, it is possible that there are tunnels nearby? But what sort of religion was practised there? If it was pagan it is quite likely that some form of sacrificial rites were carried out, and this could well affect the surrounding atmosphere. It is also surprising how many tales exist of nuns being bricked up or buried alive in convents. Traditionally, it was claimed that they were punished by this method for some such misdemeanour as falling in love with a monk, but many such incarcerations in cells were entirely voluntary. Closed communities, such as religious orders, must contain an amazing concentration of deep thought. In accordance with our basic theory of the creation of ghosts, it is easy to imagine some old inmate, having spent almost the whole of his life within the confines of a monastery, unable to think of anything unconnected with his life there. Whether he died in the monastery or not is immaterial: his whole consciousness is centred within the building.

Don't abandon further research if you find that the original building was not devoted to human habitation. All buildings are associated with humans in some way. Farm buildings, barns and similar constructions are visited by people and contain objects cared for by owners.

There are a few haunted barns in the country: one of them is the site of a murder in the 19th century, and in another the suicide of a young girl is the cause of the phenomena. Some day, no doubt, the foundations of the barns will be built over, and problems created for the occupants of the new property.

The case of a ghostly cow in an open field in Monmouth must be unique, but it is well attested, having been seen over a period of many months by several independent witnesses. One can only assume that this particular animal was a pet of the original farmer or herdsman, and when it died, or was killed, the phantom was created in the same way as are the ghosts of many domestic animals. More usually and understandably these consist mainly of cats, dogs and horses, though the occasional ghost of a rabbit is reported.

Phantom birds appear only to be linked with death warnings and their prevalence was on the wane by the end of the 19th century. Ghosts of sheep are unknown, but stories of an apparition of a blue donkey circulated in Cobham in the early 1960s. It was established that this had been created by a former clown, who owned the donkey and had painted it blue to aid his own performance in a travelling circus during the previous century. When the animal died he was naturally very upset.

Since numerous buildings are likely to have been constructed on one specific site, it is a good idea to fit transparent overlays, one for each period of occupation, on to the basic plan of the site. This has been done to great advantage by archaeologists, for by this means the general development and change of outlines over the years can be shown. The transparent overlays may well explain the phenomenon of a "cold spot", which could be a well-covered over some years previously. An alternatively method is to draw a plan of the building with a key for each period of construction, as shown in fig. 11.

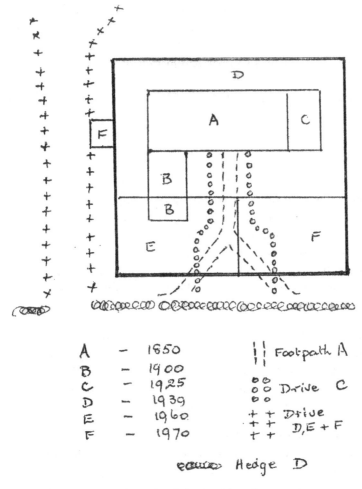

A   –   1850   ¦¦ Footpath A
B   –   1900
C   –   1925   ∘∘ Drive C
D   –   1939   ∘∘
E   –   1960   ++ Drive
F   –   1970   ++   D, E + F

Hedge D

Fig. 11 - PLAN SHOWING HISTORICAL DEVELOPMENT OF A BUILDING

As an alternative to establishing "what was there before" in order to link some incident with a current haunting, it could be just as interesting to try and find out why a ghost no longer haunts although all the symptoms indicate that it should. Was the former property exorcised, thus breaking the regenerative continuity needed, if so by whom, when and what type of phenomena called for this action?

Exorcism may work in some instances, but fairly frequently a ghost which has undergone this rite returns in a following generation. Perhaps a younger member of the family which witnessed the apparition, who was not present during the service, will continue to see the phantom.

A case which occurred in Yorkshire during 1971 demonstrates the need to check and re-check information concerning the history of an area. Workmen demolishing an old building to make way for a new office block stated that they had seen the ghost of a Quaker within feet of an old tombstone that was being moved. So distinct was the figure that a sketch was made of the apparition on the stone by one of the team. He was sure, it was reported, that it was a Quaker because the old house used to be owned by a religious group "many years ago" before it became derelict and was sold for development.

In fact, the building had been owned by a Jewish group and the figure was that of a Rabbi, not a Quaker. The obtaining of accurate information made it possible to identify the apparition in question, and from this it may be possible to find out why the figure haunts the site, for there are not many reports of Jewish ghosts. It is doubtful in this particular case that the new tenants of the offices will experience any phenomena, but it is the sort of incident that should occasionally be checked up on, just to see if the phenomena have recurred.

In cases of historical houses, especially those open to the public, there is so much information available that they may be considered as ideal starting points for the new investigator. But be warned: the published data is not always accurate, so a ghost-hunter may easily be misled especially where names of individuals and dates are concerned.

Historical information regarding public houses, not surprisingly favourite spots to start ghost-hunting, can often be obtained from the brewers. But, again, it is wise to check with local specialists.

Much interesting and valuable material can be obtained regarding local history by a visit to the library; if the case is situated in a fairly large town, there may also be an information or tourist centre which supplies maps and brochures or a local records office. Many records and archives are in the process of being digitalised, particularly in the field of family history and a computerised register of burials in Great Britain is available. The archives of the longer-established psychical research societies may also contain earlier reports of activity at a particular site, in the form of newspaper articles, correspondence or reports from previous investigators.

A haunt in Gloucestershire further demonstrates the need for care and accuracy. A phantom in Cavalier uniform riding a huge white horse, according to local legend, is a messenger to the Royalist troops waiting to take part in one of the battles of the Civil War (1642-1646). The two apparitions have been seen moving rapidly across a field which residents claim "was the site of the old road to the battle site". Archaeologists agree that evidence proves there was most certainly a path through what is now agricultural land, but early maps also prove that it was dug up long before the Civil War, and had been put under the plough at least 100 years before Cromwell was born.

This mixture of scraps of genuine information and incorrect dates is fairly commonly encountered, and a pitfall to watch for. Individuals can be vague about dates of even recent events, and in some cases stories that noises were heard "a few years ago" can, in fact, be a much longer time - nearly fifty years in some cases. Don't be deceived, either, into assuming that all official information need never be questioned.

The curator of a National Trust property in a genuine attempt to help with one case of a haunting advised me that the ghost was that of a Mrs. Carruthers who had died after a second marriage in 1710. Perhaps it was as well that I scrutinised the published history of the property, for it showed that the lady in question was still a widow in 1712 and remarried in 1722. She died in 1745, and therefore the ghost reported in 1734 was either someone else altogether or a ghost of the living; or maybe the published records are wrong.

An example of how just inaccurate popular accounts of alleged hauntings can prove to be shown is illustrated by one investigator's study of the haunting of Igtham Mote in Kent, an ancient building haunted by the phantom of an early 17th century resident of the house, Dame Mary Selby. According to published accounts she was responsible for betraying Guy Fawkes and the conspirators behind the Gunpowder Plot of 1605 and suffered death by being walled-up in an act of revenge by the surviving Catholic plotters, and that her skeleton is concealed in the house. This tale of murder has been endlessly served up as a fact in popular books proposing it as the explanation for the (slight) evidence of a haunting at the site. However, one investigator on a visit to the site decided to conduct some preliminary checks and on going to the local church found it to contain Dame Selby's tomb. Information at the church also established that far from being walled-up alive, Dame Selby had gone on to live another 36 years after the failure of the Gunpowder Plot, eventually dying a natural death.[31] Wherever possible you should seek to trace the earliest source or account of a story, whether published or unpublished, since distortions may arise with the written word, as much as information repeated orally.

To return to the question of the haunting of uninhabited property: I heard of an incident that may well account for a ghost that "just vanishes into thin air at the bottom of the garden." Since apparitions will walk through walls because they were constructed after the thought picture was created, it is probably not entirely surprising to learn that the reverse can happen. In the garden in question, in the Midlands, up to a few years ago an ice-house reminded locals and historians of the days before refrigerators and deep freezers. As you may know, these small buildings were constructed for storing ice used by the household during the summer months; early models were made of earth and covered with shrubs to ensure the preservation of the cold atmosphere. Later, more expensive types were built on brick or stone, or both.

Early in the 1970s, when developers built a small block of flats on the site of a mansion, the ice-house, for no apparent reason, was demolished. It was many feet away from the property and could not have interfered in any way with the construction of the new homes. Anyway, the ghost who used to visit the little building, which was about eleven feet long, obviously still calls in: he is now seen to disappear "into thin air", for he has nowhere else to go. The creation of the phantom may have stemmed from an accident in which a pony fell into a building – the floor of some are as low as seven feet below ground level. The problem of getting the valuable animal out of its predicament was solved by feeding in bales of straw through a side aperture, until the pony was high enough to walk out scared but unharmed.

Other old buildings which would attract a visit by someone at some time, but which would be unlikely to remain in existence for longer than the associated property, include wells, privies, conservatories and even tool-sheds. There are a few haunted wells, the sites of which I presume will remain affected by phenomena long after the reason for their presence has been forgotten; but I must admit that I only know of one outside lavatory that boasts of a ghost, and this used to be a workshop and is quite modern.

An ancient public house in Lincolnshire called the Bluebell Inn originally obtained its water from a thirty-foot deep well in the back of the courtyard.

---

[31] Fraser, John (2012) *Ghost Hunting: A Survivor's Guide*. UK. History Press.

Because of the obvious danger presented by the open well it was bricked up some years ago, but a "shadowy figure" is still seen late at night moving across the yard and bending down over the former well-head. No doubt when the existence of the well is forgotten and the site destroyed locals will be mystified by the ghost which vanishes in the middle of, perhaps, a car park.

Sites of conservatories, lean-tos, and greenhouses may well be haunted by horticultural enthusiasts but, unfortunately for the researcher there is very unlikely to be any sign of them on maps or documents. The investigator would have to rely on memory or site examination for signs of foundations or heating pipes.

Stables may well contain phantom horses or, as in a couple of cases, the smell of them, despite having been converted to garages. Ghostly smells are not unusual. In my own house visitors used to comment on the odour of pipe tobacco, which was experienced occasionally in the evening. I had never smoked a pipe in the house until January 1972 and neither had anyone else for at least five years before then. This smell could be caused by wind blowing down the chimney at a certain angle and stirring up some of the 250-year-old soot which lies in it. Two former owners, one of whom was killed in a car crash within feet of the front gate – the other committed suicide in a nearby river - both smoked clay pipes, remnants of which I have found in the garden.

Two establishments in London, one a dental surgery and the other a historic building in Chiswick, are both affected by the tantalizing odour of frying eggs and bacon. Both of these are claimed to be reminders of the days when kitchens were in the buildings. The kitchens at Chiswick were removed over 100 years ago and the nearest building is over half a mile away. Again, wind from a certain angle in the chimney could be the answer, but without daily tests, it would be impossible to confirm this idea.

The smell of a snuffed out candle is experience at midnight in a farm in Lancashire. One wonders if there is oil-fired central heating there, for the smell of paraffin wax which was another derivative of crude oil, is not unlike that of heating oil.

Smells in outside localities can be just as peculiar. Perfume can be detected outside the sitting-room of a large farmhouse in Kent, and "the smell of the grave" pervades a spinney in Savernake Forest. Legend has it that a murdered body was buried at the spot among the trees, but no-one seems to have bothered, or dared, to find out if this belief is true. Logical reasons for these phenomena are left to the reader to deduce, but might I suggest a decaying animal (a fox or a deer) in the latter case, and the possibility of a buried perfume bottle in the former. Or is there a perfume factory nearby, the drains from which lie close to the house or are linked with its drains?

A case of poltergeist activity not associated with an adolescent received a lot of press coverage during 1971. The premises are those of an art centre a few miles from Dublin. Not only were objects thrown around but an intense feeling of evil pervaded the building and a "huge black cat" haunted a corridor. The centre was exorcised, but the relief from the troubles was only temporary, and they recommenced a few months later. The area is well known for its association with the Hell-Fire Club, a branch of the notorious group in High Wycombe which was formed by a band of young rakes in the 18th century.[32]

According to one sufferer from the phenomena, the remains of a young male dwarf, one of the victims of the Club's activities, were found within feet of the Arts Centre a few years ago. It is this sort of information that needs checking all along the line. Where are the remains now? Who was present when they were found? How can one establish that the bones were those of a dwarf and not of a child? Was there an inquest? Why is the assumption made that the remains were those of a victim of the Hell-Fire Club? Is there any real evidence to support this? Etc., etc?

Although the building is "known to be associated with Sir Francis Dashwood", what evidence exists to confirm this? I am not suggesting that this particular case is probably fraudulent – in fact I have good reason to suppose that it is genuine – I am merely quoting it as an example to indicate what sort of information would assist in authenticating the details given.

In 1972 nearly 120 cases of hauntings were reported, and of these some 25% were recorded as "repeat incidents". This percentage of cases with a previous history is on the increase, and it is for this reason that records are essential: not only the complete history of the particular case but also information about the immediate locality and its surroundings.

An incident at Salford, Lancashire, demonstrates this need. The *Manchester Evening News* reported on the 25th February 1972 that the Victoria Theatre there, which was then being turned into a Bingo Hall, has a long history of

---

[32] Green, Andrew (1973) *Our Haunted Kingdom*. UK.Wolfe Publications.

haunting by a female apparition. The ghost has been seen to "come through the bar through one wall and disappear through another". Other phenomena, such as a door being opened inexplicably, were also experienced. Next door to the theatre lies the Irwell Castle Hotel, separated by only a narrow wall from the Victoria, and this is also affected by a phantom. The head and shoulders of a figure are claimed to have been seen "coming into the building through a back wall".

I don't know if this particular dual haunting is interconnected, but it is the type of incident that needs clarification and full investigation. Who is the theatrical apparition? Does the description match that given by witnesses in the hotel? When was the partitioning wall built? Were the two buildings one? These are but a few of the questions to which answers would be needed for the final report.

In 1970, at an oil-refinery in Essex, I interviewed a witness who had, some 24 hours earlier, seen the apparition of "a thick-set man in a steel helmet" walking along a service road within the area of the works near some cleaning tanks. This was the second time that the worker had seen a ghost within his lifetime, and he was, surprisingly, as scared then as he had been on the previous occasion (some thirty years earlier).

The description he gave of the night-walking phantom roughly matched that of a man known to have died fifteen years earlier in one of the tanks. This case seems to fall into the "haunting apparition" classification, for it had been seen without previous knowledge by the man I interviewed, and on a couple of other occasions by other people; and the witness had no idea that the figure he saw was that of a worker who had died in the locality some years ago.

In Sandy Lane, Dereham, Norfolk the phantom of a man was seen by a cyclist "walking" about a foot above the ground; some two years later the same figure was seen by a woman as she was walking home one night. During 1973 it was found that a teenager had also seen the apparition, and was able to describe it as "a tall man in knee-length breeches, long stockings and a long shirt". The figure she had seen, however, was in a room in one of the houses in the lane. The description tallies with the other sightings in 1972 in the road (one can, I think, safely assume that the level of the road was lowered many years ago).

With a certain amount of research in the library, in the highway department of the local Council and in the rating office, one should be able to find out the age of the houses, when the road level was altered and who had lived in the properties. In the UK official information held by local and national government covering records held by a wide variety of state agencies and bodies can also be obtained through the Freedom of Information Act 2000. Since enactment this has provided a source of information on matters relating to paranormal reports made to the police and official bodies.[33] Careful questioning of the witness should make it possible to obtain a better description of the apparition in order to identify it. A study of the church register would probably reveal the names of people who might fit the description and who died during the period involved. The cause of death may also be given. (There is no reason to suppose that the figure in this case is that of a living person).

Examination of the information obtained from the witnesses, of which there seem to be at least four, should indicate whether they had any previous knowledge concerning the haunting, for this could well affect the descriptions given. As to the method of interviewing and questioning, a later chapter will provide some advice and assistance but from the sample cases given here readers may perhaps appreciate the underlying object of the careful investigation and close study of all factors involved in a case of haunting.

It should not be forgotten that local police can be extremely helpful in a lot of cases, especially where poltergeist incidents or those associated with witchcraft are involved. They can be a mine of information when it comes to general local gossip – but never divulge the source of this information. Confidence is not always easy to win and should never be broken. If you can establish a friendly relationship with the local police at the outset of an investigation it may prove to be extremely valuable in future cases. When people are scared by phenomena, the local police station is sometimes the first place they think of running for help. The image of matter-of-fact calmness and common sense projected by the police goes a long way to soothe upset nerves and hysterical witnesses. Members of the local community in other roles such as the church or voluntary organisations such as the Women's Institute can also be a source of information, though often this has to be assessed with care and not taken at face value. Often this information may stray into folkloric territory where it cannot be checked or corroborated or sources are not given or recalled.

---

[33] In the UK made under the Freedom of Information Act 2000, section 1.

A case of what sounded like old witchcraft attracted the attention of a local research group in Ipswich during August 1972. At Fakenham Magna builders restoring a group of cottages heard footsteps and mysterious tappings after they had revealed mummified remains of a couple of cats in the building. When the foreman of the team took the bodies back home to show his family, his wife began to hear unusual noises in the kitchen, which she attributed to the dead cats. In the hope that the phenomena would cease, the workman asked for the bodies of the animals to be brought back to the cottages. Reporters from *Bury Free Press* on visiting the site admitted that they had heard inexplicable footsteps, and claimed that the air inside the buildings was "unnaturally hot".[34]

By retaining mummified or preserved "familiars" whether they were frogs, toads, lizards or cats, witches would be able to keep their powers – or so it was believed in olden times. This fact, possibly known by one of the witnesses, could well be the basic reason for the phenomena; it would be interesting to find out if the original owners of the cottages, which were built in the 17th century, had the reputation of being connected with magic.

---

[34] *Bury Free Press* 8 August 1972. Murdie, Alan (2008) *Haunted Bury St Edmunds*. UK. Tempus Books.

CHAPTER 7

History of the affected premises

This subject may appear to be dealing with matters similar to those discussed in the previous chapter, but in fact what we are concerned with here is in the immediate past history of the building, rather than details that can only be found in libraries and ancient records. The details obtained in some cases will act as confirmation of those already obtained.

It is a good idea to find out from the present residents the names of previous occupants of the property. It may be that they were friends, relatives or acquaintances. Details of who they were and what they did all help to build a complete picture of the circumstances surrounding the haunting.

A fictional case may help to clarify the reasons for this sort of enquiry. A private house appears to be haunted, and one of the major incidents is that electric lights come on and off without any apparent reason. Although one should obviously check the whole wiring system and ascertain its age at the same time, information in addition that the previous owner was an electrician, or (even more relevant) an amateur electrician, would naturally make one a little suspicious and could well account for the peculiar effects.

How long has the current owner been in residence? This point is extremely important, for many cases occur where people have just moved into strange new surroundings. After about a year they have usually settled in, and have begun to realise that the many noises and lights that at first they regarded as "psychic phenomena" are in fact quite normal incidents.

Poltergeist activity is a phenomenon often experienced within days of moving, especially into Council property. The possible cause, an adolescent about the age of puberty usually being responsible for such phenomena, is the mental turmoil created in the young mind. A completely new neighbourhood, probably a whole new way of living – all have to be coped with. Little calming influence is received from the parents at this time, as they too are undergoing the upheaval of the routines and behaviour patterns. Pre-occupied with sorting things out and getting some semblance of order back into their lives, they tend to ignore the youngster or tell them that he or she is "in the way" or "being a nuisance", until the concentrated mental stress can be contained no longer and breaks out in the form of poltergeist activity. The adolescent is attempting subconsciously to re-assert his position in the household. In a case of a poltergeist outbreak or more a lengthy haunting one should also note who is the first person in the household to report experiencing phenomena as such an individual may play a key role in the events, whatever their causation.

If the witnesses are long-established in the property, check on whether any recent alterations have been made to the structure, such as the installation of central heating. If so, establish what sort of system it is. Gas can sometimes smell of sulphur, while oil, as we have seen, may give rise to reports of "burning candles". Paraffin heaters and blow-torches, incidentally, may be the source of similar stories, so if there has been any decorating carried out recently check on what tools were used.

If any demolition has taken pace, such as the removal of a wall, a doorway, a fireplace or an outbuilding, the site as it was before should be recorded on your sketch plan and the reasons for the work ascertained. You should also establish whether any unusual object or item of interest was found during the course of the work and, if so, whether the witness of the haunting knew about this. Was the object involved in any way linked with the haunting? A brooch found in an old fireplace or under the floor-boards may have been lost for years and could be the cause of the apparition. The finding of a tombstone is almost certainly significant; and perhaps the carving knife discovered in an ancient baking-oven is associated with the inexplicable moans issuing from the adjoining chimney? Now that what may have been a weapon has been exposed will the "hauntings" stop, and if so why? Or perhaps the moaning started when the knife was found?

Many people seem to think that structural alterations, especially those in an old building, are the cause of the phenomena being experienced. A young man I interviewed in Surrey assured me that the "weird light on the landing" and "the popping sound like a table-tennis ball" were due to his removing a wall in the sitting room of his terraced Victorian home. So convinced was he of this explanation that he decided to organise a séance, even though he had "banished the ghostie" by swearing at it. The fact that he had only moved in six weeks earlier, and has a young daughter who was obviously affected by all the activity, was "nothing to do with it".

The Compstons, licensees of the New Inn at Foulridge, were convinced that the cause of three flower-pots crashing to the floor from a window sill was some alterations being made to the premises in February 1972. A previous landlord, Mr. Harrison, said that similar phenomena were experienced in the 1960s when he was having "some changes made"; although, to quote the *Colne Times*, "there is a history of haunting" there of a peculiar nature. Here again there is an association with the dead, for an old Quaker's graveyard forms the garden on the west side of the New Inn. Tombstones were in fact used in the wall surrounding the plot.

One visual incident was a "luminous cross", which was seen on the ceiling of a small bedroom by a couple of young brothers; but it is not known whether anyone attempted a serious investigation to find out the cause of this occurrence. The possibility of a reflection from the glass or some other shiny object cannot be ruled out in this instance.

Have the premises been subject to any flooding in living memory? Months after the river Wey broke its banks in Surrey householders complained of "weird footsteps", "creaks", "groaning", and of course, "peculiar smells" in the houses which were drying out after the flood waters had subsided. New owners of such property, having of course no previous knowledge of the havoc caused by the flooding, could well be justifiably apprehensive concerning the phenomena.

You should try to establish as tactfully as possible, the names, addresses and occupations of people who regularly visit the household, and, if the haunting is a new one, the identity of the last person to call before it started. It is possible that a call from an unexpected visitor will "spark off" phenomena, especially if the caller, during the course of the conversation, expressed an interest in the subject of ghosts and the supernatural. If a child is in the household enquire as to whether he or she was present at the time the topic was raised. The answer could be of interest, especially if it contains a description of the child's general attitude to the discussion.

Have there been any recent violent or sudden deaths associated either with the property or with the occupants? If so, the investigator should obviously obtain as much detail as possible for checking and verifying later.

One case illustrating the need for this type of information occurred at a hundred-year-old council house in Halton Bank, Salford, Lancashire. Only two weeks after a couple with their six children moved in, poltergeist phenomena commenced. Light bulbs fell to the floor for no apparent reason and without breaking, water taps were turned on and the gas oven was found to have the taps wide open on two occasions. But the parents have seen the apparition of an old man in the house, an incident apparently unconnected with the psychokinesis. One enquiry it was learnt that the former tenants had also seen the ghost. A neighbour who has been resident in the area for some forty years stated that the description of the phantom matched that of a man who died very suddenly and rather mysterious, after a "very full and active life".

A rather unusual incident connected with the discovery of tombs was reported in the *Yarmouth Mercury* in June 1972. When excavations for a new fire station on Friars Lane were nearing completion a stone coffin was discovered which contained two skeletons. This was widely reported and was believed to be one of the few burials connected with the 15th century monastery which had formerly stood on the site.

Shortly after the new station was officially opened, firemen began to experience strange whistlings and scampering footsteps. The local paper stated that an elderly woman who, when a child, had lived in a house which formed part of the site, had claimed that "numerous apparitions were seen at this time". These not only included the expected figures of monks, but also the apparitions of a woman and girl, and these were always preceded by a peculiar whistling. Other phenomena experienced in the house consisted of the movement of the furniture, the opening of doors and the rattling of a poker. How much of this detail was previously known to the firemen who experienced the phenomena is an unanswered question.

If the ghost is of a pet animal you should try to find out who owned such a creature, when, and the date it died or was killed. This could prove to be an impossible task, but the local police may be able to point to a record of the incident if a dog was a victim of a car accident.

A tragedy which obviously affected the atmosphere of a house in Collyhurst, Lancashire occurred in March 1970 when a Mrs Potter was stabbed to death in her flat in Northern Drive. This cause of death is often likely to create a ghost. The unfortunate victim has time just before death to see the attackers striking the final blows, and to visualise himself writhing in his death-throes. As a result of this appalling murder (for some reason I always feel that stabbing is more horrific than shooting) a family are badly affected by the apparition which haunts the flat. So upset were they when they first experienced it that the two children, aged five and three, were taken to the local hospital suffering from severe shock.

Another Manchester case, in which a married teen-aged couple are involved, provides a demonstration of the assumption made by witnesses that "voices" are directed at them. The eighteen-year old wife has been scared by hearing someone "unseen" calling on her to "wake up". The couple have already been scared by doors opening and the sound of "phantom footsteps". Presuming that this report is genuine, I find it difficult to accept that this ghost is unique in being able to converse orally. But I am prepared to believe that someone at some time had cause to call out the command for some urgent reason – perhaps a fire in the house. A more mundane explanation is that the "creator" of the ghost was so used to this routine each morning that his subconscious created the permanent "record" in the atmosphere.

A Dorset case of apparent haunting that I know could well involve auto-suggestion. The site involved a public house in Lyme Regis sited practically on the river Lynn, has had a long reputation for being haunted by a former owner, a woman dressed like Queen Victoria. According to my informant, the lady in question gave up the licence of the pub in 1927 because her daughter's drinking habits were affecting the profits; but before leaving the landlady stated to all and sundry that "no-one will ever do as well as I did". All licensees since then "have suffered in some way and the 'curse' has been proved". Some of the incidents over a forty-five year period have included the breaking-up of two happy marriages, the absconding by a landlord with the Christmas club funds, and later the sudden death of a landlord. The licence was then held by his widow.

A local retailer, who had been offered the pub but refused it "because of its history" and his "own experiences there, told me that he had seen the "phantom of the old lady" He was reluctant to provide, further details, for they might recall the frightening incident more vividly, and he had also been scared by something else "which came out of a cupboard".

Studying this information in the cold light of reason we find that there is really very little evidence of a haunting at all. One would expect a mixture of landlords and deaths over a period of forty-five years, and the cases are not in any way out of the ordinary. The witnessing of the "phantom" can hardly be classed as paranormal until further and fuller details of the two incidents are known. The man in question had known about the story of the woman for many years, having worked with his father in the pub. The "thing in the cupboard" could well have been a pet animal accidentally shut in.

I am not trying to dismiss what could be a perfectly genuine case, but merely pointing out that the information obtained in this case is far from sufficient on which to base a file. How old is the property? Why should the old woman haunt the building? Perhaps she "willed" herself into the atmosphere to act as a disturbing influence on following owners; or, more likely, she was quite happy there and highly annoyed that her daughter's behaviour had forced her to leave. Is the close proximity of the river in any way connected with the haunting? When was the apparition seen? Has anyone else witnessed it? There are a host of questions which need answering before one can even consider this a possible authentic haunting.

Another haunted building with a long history of phenomena is the Pier Theatre in Shanklin, Isle of Wight; but whether it can be classified as genuine or not is open to doubt, for many people must know the story and have heard the description of the phantom.

The musical director, Mr John Carr, accepted that the phenomena of doors mysteriously opening and the movement of objects was due to the death on the stage of an actor in 1898. By now hundreds of people know what he looks like, for his description was published in the *Daily Express* in July 1972. Several witnesses claim that the figure is of "a white-haired man with mutton chop sideboards, a high-necked suit with a grey cravat and a diamond pin." It is very seldom that one obtains such clear details from witnesses.

I would certainly be natural to assume that the ghost is that of the actor, but does the description *really* match? What is the connection, if any, with the cold spot situated in one particular seat in the theatre about which some customers complain?

Stately homes open to the public usually contain a family so well documented and recorded that it would be unwise to pester the owner for details which are usually easily obtainable from published works. The ghost however, may not be so well publicised, and the enquirer may well find a discrepancy between the information provided by the witness and the published record. This situation will necessitate a certain amount of research, but it should be comparatively easy to clarify.

What may be a little more troublesome is the "new" ghost which sometimes crops up in a property open to the public. Woburn Abbey has had a couple since the owners opened up new sections to the public, and in 1972 a visitor to the Tower of London described what she thought was a fresh case; in fact her description of the apparition turned out to match that of one of the well known ghosts. It is sometimes difficult to carry out a full scale investigation in premises open to the public, for special arrangement would obviously have to be made, and owners are naturally not particularly happy at opening up "after hours".

Hotels fall into a somewhat different category, although here too there may be problems. If the manager or owner of a hotel has already advised the press of the phenomena an approach from a serious investigator may be welcomed. One such case could be the Park Hotel at Falkirk in Scotland, where the sounds of a car and footsteps on the gravel have disturbed the staff. "Phantom footsteps" are also heard inside the building. Rumours accounting for these phenomena tend to suggest that a girl who went missing from the house some twenty years before and a secret underground passage were the combined cause. One of the most peculiar series of incidents, some of which were discussed on site by a BBC television team from the *Twenty-Four Hours* programme, occurred at the Palace Hotel, Southport, in 1969. The principal phenomenon was that a four ton lift moved up and down the shaft by itself despite the fact, confirmed by North Wales Electricity Board who carried out their own investigation, that "there isn't an amp of power going into the place". All electricity had been cut off from the site *weeks* before the team of workmen arrived to demolish the old 1,000 room building.

The second floor of the building appeared to be the centre of activity, for the lift would glide up from ground to the second floor and then stop. A dog brought in by the BBC to "test the atmosphere" refused to pass the landing on the second floor, but had no objection to any of the others. In order to stop the movement of the lift it was found necessary not merely to cut the cables and the main shafts, but to hit the unit for nearly half an hour with 28lb hammers to cause it to plunge down into the cellars. Although the experience must have been disturbing, no cause was ever found in for this genuine phenomena.

Nearly a year later, in April 1970, a "mysterious fire" started in an oil tank and a bulldozer was capsized; no mean feat for anybody, let alone a ghost. It will be interesting to watch for reports of any haunting in the future on this site.

A point about this particular case is that there seems to be no explanation at all for the incidents, apart from a rumour (and it was only a rumour) that a woman had committed suicide on the second floor about thirty or forty years before. If it is true that the effects of this tragedy could affect a four ton lift, then it would seem that the power of psychokinesis must be regarded as such that no object is too heavy to move. If this principle becomes generally accepted it could account for the phenomena.

The question of establishing the history of a haunted school can lead to problems, for although the principal may be willing to provide details, s/he will often be reluctant to allow any deep research into the phenomena. This situation calls for the maximum amount of tact, and even then it is doubtful if permission for a thorough investigation will be given, unless disturbance by poltergeist activity obviously demands some form of action, or the constant visitation of a "phantom" is a severe problem.

It is likely, I think, that schools, convents and similar establishments will prove to be the sites of more poltergeist activity than "normal" phenomena, although I admit there are at least three boarding schools and five universities that are reputed to be haunted by "ghosts". In one case a previous pupil is believed to be the phantom, but because the identity cannot be established it is not possible to ascertain whether this is just another "ghost of the living". This explanation could account for many incidents in houses of learning, for people are often apt to reflect, sometimes with deep intensity, on the days of their childhood and youth which were spent in such establishments.

It would be unusual for a non-boarding school to be affected by phenomena, unless the history of the building showed it was the site of some other type of establishment. But I know of two youth clubs which appear to be haunted; the phantoms are those of people who lived on the premises when they were private houses.

The history of cinemas and theatres is usually well documented, so when discussing phenomena experienced on the premises with managers or proprietors, it is more important to establish details of recent accidents and the identities of regular patrons. Old age pensioners are apt to use cinemas a lot, for special price reductions tempt many old people to indulge in a few hours of relaxation, and these are not always spent watching the film. It may therefore be well worth while to talk to local pensioners in cases of cinema hauntings.

Chapter 8

Interviewing the witness and procedures to adopt

Extracting a detailed description of the phenomena from the witness is the whole basis of an investigation, but there are many aspects to this exercise. Having made an appointment at a time convenient to the witness, stress the fact that his or her name will not be published without consent. Normally this is given straight away, but point out the context in which you may wish to mention it, and this may help with the reluctant individual. There are other aspects concerning publicity which I will cover later.

Never attend an interview without your camera, fitted for flash, and the thermometer. Even if no phenomena occur while you are with the witness it is vital to photograph the site, if possible under conditions similar to those prevailing when the original incident occurred.

The ghost hunter, like any good detective should never "lead the witness". Never suggest things or put words into his/her mind. Some witnesses will volunteer a lot of information and talk with a minimum of questioning or prompting, whilst others may be less forthcoming and shy about sharing details. Try to be methodical with the questions, and record the witness's statement either by written notes or on tape. Always first ask permission to use a tape-recorder, and explain that the recording will be confidential, though you may wish to extract portions of it for your report. As stated earlier, once the machine is switched on, try to forget it. Put it on a table and treat it as part of the furniture, to be ignored until required.

Having noted the sex and approximate age of the witness, you should also record whether spectacles are worn, and if so, for how long, and whether they are bi-focals. Establish whether contact lenses are worn, if the eyesight has been checked recently, and whether the witness is colour-blind. It may be necessary at this stage to point out that you are not suggesting that anything is wrong with the statement of the witness; but the report will be read by people who have not had the opportunity of meeting the person involved, and it is therefore essential to retain a professional approach.

It is important to identify as accurately as possible the date of the experiences. Obviously, the more recent the experience, the more likely the witness is to be remembering it accurately. The passage of time inevitably leads people to forget details – even something as remarkable as seeing a ghost! There is also the risk that as details become hazy and forgotten there may be a tendency to invent information or dramatise what occurred, consciously or subconsciously and even to fantasise about what occurred in the interests of "a good story". Stories may become wildly exaggerated with popular retellings in folklore and in the press but this can also happen on an individual level.

It is important to gain at least a general impression of the health of the witness. If s/he has recently seen a doctor or is currently receiving treatment, try to elicit further details. If the treatment involves taking tranquilizers, it could well affect the whole case, especially if the witness's account of the phenomena experienced is unsubstantiated by others. As there appears to be some link between epilepsy and the experiencing of paranormal phenomena, enquire (tactfully) if there is any history in the family of this disease.

All these questions may appear at first sight to be unnecessarily probing and I am not suggesting that one should ask all of them in every case. One must, however, be prepared for every type of incident, and the questions are given to provide an indication of the kind of information required. It is necessary for the parapsychologist to employ some kind of psychological approach.

However, if you suspect mental illness you should not attempt to diagnose this yourself and leave it to those qualified to work in the area of mental health. Whilst the recognition of subjective distress on the part of the witness is a significant issue in an investigation, responding to it correctly should be left to a practitioner with the expertise to do it, whether he or she is a clinical psychologist, a social worker, a trained counsellor or a doctor.[35] Making irresponsible claims about occult or psychic influences being at work can inflict serious harm on the mental state of a witness and you should avoid making any casual remarks that might suggest to a witness that malevolent ghosts or evil spirits are present. Unfortunately, as with fraudulent mediums, there have also been cases of wholly fraudulent psychic investigators who recklessly make such claims, sometimes as a ruse to extract money from a vulnerable person for supposedly getting rid of an alleged entity that has no existence outside imagination. The amount of

---

[35] McHarg, J,(1982) 'The Paranormal and the Recognition of Personal Distress,' in *Journal of the Society for Psychical Research* Vol 51, 1982, pp. 201-9 ; Wim H. Kramer, Eberhard Bauer, and Gerd H. Hovelmann (2012) *Perspectives of Clinical Parapsychology: An Introductory Reader.*

psychological harm that can be done to a vulnerable person by the reckless promotion of fanciful and fantastic claims should not be underestimated.[36]

Remember that more women see ghosts than men, or at least more reports are received from women. This may be due to the fact that women generally have more time available in which to experience phenomena; or that women are more sensitive or have more vivid imaginations; or (perhaps an old-fashioned suggestion) that they are more emotional than men and are therefore endowed with a lesser degree of logic.

When asking about the witness's employment, find out not only what sort of work s/he does but also whether s/he is really happy at it. Boredom can cause imagination to run riot. Even if the automatic reply of "it's all right" is offered, pursue the matter and dig a little deeper in order to find out the witness's real attitude to his/her job. How many hours a day are worked, is it on a repetitive factory line, is it dull office routine which s/he dislikes; or, in contrast, is it varied, exciting and interesting? If the work is part-time, how does the witness occupy the remainder of the day? Those who are mentally busy, and I mean *mentally*, obviously have a different outlook to those merely carrying out the dull routine of household chores. A mind fully occupied will be both less susceptible to imagination and more receptive to the unexpected incident.

A lady in the lounge of her flat in Littleborough, Lancashire, was quietly dusting the ornaments one day, "not thinking of anything in particular", when, on turning to pick up some knitting, she noticed that one of her vases appeared to be missing. She moved towards the spot where it should have been and realised that the phantom of a woman in a black dress was standing in front of the vase hiding it from view. The tenant, astonished, looked at the figure "for about two minutes", and it faded away. What the thoughts of the lady actually were while she was dusting is not known, but they could perhaps have been on the ghost of a "friendly female in grey" which had already been reported by other tenants.

Another lady I had the pleasure of meeting in her magnificent house near Ashford, Kent, told me that when making up a bed in one of the guest bedrooms one afternoon she heard a noise behind her, and, on turning, saw her transistor radio "rise from the top of the dressing table" about eight feet

---

[36] Green, Andrew (1977) correspondence in *Journal of the Society for Psychical Research* Vol 49 No 771. This highlighted a case in Birmingham Andrew Green investigated in 1976 where a family had been defrauded by psychics claiming the house was haunted.

away, move slowly towards her and "finally come to rest on the side of the bed" furthest from her. At the time she had been wondering about the progress of reconstruction work being carried out on the ground floor: but I wonder if the incident was a case of psychokinesis. It is possible that subconsciously she had thought of a particular programme on the radio, or had needed the sound of music to relieve the silence of the house. We shall never be certain of the answer.

Experiencing phenomena, as has been remarked before, often seems to be connected in some way with sexual frustration; it may well be tactless and unwise to enquire deeply about this subject, but it should be noted if the witness is living alone, or if his or her partner appears uncommunicative or lethargic. This is another good reason for paying a return visit, for moods and attitudes frequently change: a witness who appeared at first to be a solemn, even gloomy individual may turn out to be a lively person full of humour and gaiety.

Ascertain the general atmosphere in the household. Is it tense or homely? Are the people involved nervous and on edge or calm and at ease? All these factors help to create a general picture of the foundation on which to build a case.

Obtain if you can, a complete minute-by-minute description of the phenomena. In Chapter 10 there are some reminders about questions to raise, but the most important piece of information needed is exactly where your witness was standing or positioned at the time. Mark the spot on your plan of the premises. Which way was he facing, where are the windows and doors, were (if relevant) the lights switched on, is there a mirror in the room, and what was the weather like at the time? Is the witness accustomed to English weather, and more specifically, to the atmospheric conditions of the locality? (Don't ask this kind of question if the witness has lived there all his life, of course). Is the house near a main road or on a busy shopping area, and was there heavy traffic noise at the time? Note on your sketch of the premises exactly where other members of the household were when the phenomena occurred.

Even at this stage it may be possible to arrive at some conclusion as to the authenticity of the incident. If the witness shows signs of annoyance or irritation at the form of questioning this could perhaps suggest that the case is a suspicious one. But it could equally well suggest that the witness feels you are doubting his or her sincerity and common sense. Stress again that, in order to establish and confirm his belief that he has seen a ghost (or whatever the phenomenon was), it really is necessary to obtain a complete case history with as much information as possible.

An important question, which you should investigate carefully, is whether the witness has had any similar experience before. If so, then note the details; where it was, when, and what the witness was doing at the time. The incident might not have involved seeing a ghost, but could well have concerned another type of paranormal experience such as "a dream that came true". This, too, should be recorded.

Has there been any disturbing influence or incident experienced recently in the household? This might have been, for example, a divorce or death. The witness's state of mind could well be temporarily affected by this sort of event, and it is possible that the person involved may believe that s/he was partly responsible for the occurrence. This feeling, usually quite unjustified, is not unusual in the case of a sudden bereavement, and it can weigh heavily on the mind, making the victim feel it imperative that the deceased return.

If the phenomena occurred at night, probably in a bedroom, can one be sure without any doubt that the witness was fully awake when he saw the phantom? This is practically impossible to establish, but one could enquire as to whether there is any history of sleep-walking, and examine the evidence submitted to prove that the witness was fully conscious. "I know I was awake because I heard the clock strike two" cannot be treated seriously unless someone else, perhaps in the same room, can corroborate the incident. Remember that there are many well-authenticated cases of people who have been known to be asleep and dreaming with their eyes wide open at the time.

Many such experiences occur when the percipient is alone, often when resting in bed or on a sofa. Experiences vary from dream-like or unrealistic impressions to vivid and realistic figures mistaken for actual persons. The link with sleep was also made by researcher Andrew MacKenzie in 1982. He found that about one-third of apparitional experiences occurred just before or after sleep, or when the percipient was in a state of relaxation. Similar results have been reported for other types of entity experiences, and many apparitions may be connected with images occurring either when entering sleep or before becoming fully awake. Such states – known technically as 'hypnagogic' or 'hypnopompic' have been found to be common in studies of collections of reports, with one survey in 1956 placing the figure as in high as 70%. In another study by an SPR member Dr Peter Hallson some 48% of the reported ghosts had been seen either on awakening or in conditions which were conducive to sleep. However, that more than ordinary images are involved in such states is shown by the fact that more than one person may witness the same apparition, and that the same image may be perceived by different people on different occasions.[37]

Thus, it is an important question, as to whether there any other witnesses to the phenomena, and if so does their description match that of your interviewee? If an animal of the household acted as if it too had witnessed the phenomena (dogs and cats very often do), have a look at it just to check that it appears to be healthy. I don't think that parapsychologists should be expected to have much veterinary knowledge, but seeing the animal would at least confirm that it is not suffering from some obvious ailment such as fits or mange.

It may be thought advisable at the outset of the interview to find out the religious views of the witness. A good way of doing this is to ask the witness to provide information for the completion of a standard questionnaire calling for "normal data requirements": name, address, age, sex, religion, etc. Remember, however, that answers may be automatic, and "C of E" is very often given as an answer by someone who is far from being a practising Protestant; so try to establish whether the witness really *is* a believer in the faith. This could also be useful later if an exorcism is called for.

In pursuing this aspect, it may be helpful to establish during this part of the conversation whether the witness really believes in "after-life" and, if so, what s/he considers the nature of this to be. The elucidation of this may give an interesting insight into the individual's ideas. Having now experienced some phenomena, how does s/he see it in relation to his/her earlier beliefs? Does s/he, or did s/he, believe in ghosts, and if so, what is his/her definition of them? Has s/he any suggestions as to the cause of his/her recent experience? Was s/he frightened, and if so, why? This is not as so stupid a question as it may sound, as there can be many cases of fear in this context.

Ascertain the witness's real reason for reporting the experience and to whom it was initially related. Was it described because of a genuine interest

---

[37] MacKenzie, Andrew (1982) *Hauntings and Apparitions*. UK. Heinneman. For the estimate of 48% see Hallson, Peter (2002) 'Can we make progress with Apparitions?' *Paranormal Review* No. 21, 3-5, SPR. MacKenzie, Andrew (1982) *Hauntings and Apparitions*. UK. Heinneman. Haraldsson, E. (1988). 'Survey of claimed encounters with the dead; in *Omega: Journal of Death and Dying*, 19, 103-113. For the figure of 70% see Hart, Hornell (1956) 'Six Theories of Apparitions' *Proceedings* of the SPR 50, 153-239.

in the occurrence; or was it accidentally mentioned to someone who happened to report it to the press; or was the intent perhaps to get the witness's name in the paper and thus obtain publicity for his business? As the answers vary, so will your attitude of course; but don't dismiss the case which appears to have been based on a desire for publicity, as there may well have been some foundation worth investigating on which the tale was based.

Check on the witness's attitude to publicity. Mention "the press and television coverage" and asks how s/he feels about it. His/her response, whether of dislike or of pleasure can provide a real clue to his attitude. If there is an obvious desire for publicity then make certain you obtain all the facts before allowing further discussion on the point. The witness may expect you to arrange press coverage, so beware. In view of the fact that he may be a tenant and that the owner could sue you for libelling the property, I would recommend you ignore all such suggestions. Even if the witnesses are owner/occupiers, don't get involved. There are not many individuals with genuine cases of hauntings who welcome publicity, though there are a few who are prepared to accept it stoically.

I would suggest that generally speaking one should never get involved with the publicity angle; if the request is made you should suggest that the witness contacts the press direct, but warn him/her in all fairness that this might affect your attitude to the investigations that you are carrying out. Try to decide if the people involved would actually benefit from publicity.

There was a case in 1968/71 which involved regular press reports of repeated hauntings in a pub in the Midlands. On enquiry in 1972, the new tenant revealed that the reports were only made by the former licensee whenever trade was bad. No apparitions had been seen and no phenomena ever experienced except by the landlord himself, and then only after "an all night session with the bottle". But, as a result of the "assistance from the press", the trade figures always improved on publication of the information that "the ghosts were back again". It is for this reason that one should treat press reports merely as something that could be worth looking into and provide the basic lead.

It may at first appear superficial and unnecessary to enquire as to what actually convinced the witness that his experience was paranormal. But in fact this is a perfectly legitimate and sensible question to ask. During 1972 I had the interesting experience of talking to a gentleman who had been employed to act, full-time, as a ghost. And it was not in Hamlet.

His occupation in a large hut at the end of a south coast pier entailed rigging up "scaring devices" for visitors to the Haunted Gallery at 5p per head. To complete the tour of the small building the people were subjected to a vision of a phantom head. This in fact was merely a luminous mask held by the employee and waved about in pitch darkness. His theatrical performance was accompanied by ghostly moans and shrieks, which apparently caused "an average of three people a week to collapse in a state of absolute terror". What astounded the performer was that people actually paid to be sent into hysterics; he even had to take a first aid course to enable him to treat his victims. One of his last customers was a fifty-year old woman who, on her bended knees, begged him, as the ghost, to leave her in peace. A middle-aged policeman who had visited the establishment "for amusement" ended up by being treated for shock and the result was longer queues!

The devices that were constructed for the benefit of the customers, to set the scene, included wooden rollers of various sizes loosely fitted to the floor to act as "bones", a large soft mattress as "bodies", and a trap-door (which opened only two inches) to the "raging sea below". The atmosphere was created by pitch darkness and appropriately sited ultra-violet spotlights illuminating various "portions of human bodies".

It is amazing that sane individuals can have allowed common sense and logic to be dismissed so easily. A haunted building at the end of a pier in which the ghost only performed from 10 to 5.30 should have hardly been credible to the most gullible, yet the results proved otherwise.

Has the witness made any objections to your carrying out a deeper investigation involving the taking of statements from other people for purposes of corroboration? This might not only be connected with the description of the phenomena, but could also act as a sort of character reference for the original witness. It is probably unwise to let this intention be obvious.

One very important point should however be made clear to the witness: if the apparition or incident is seen or experienced again, he should keep a careful note of time and place, and, if possible, the statement should be signed and witnessed as soon as possible after the event: this means minutes and not days. Even though the witness may well promise to do this it is advisable to contact him occasionally, just to check that nothing has occurred, for people are very apt to forget promises made under these circumstances.

Has the witness any knowledge of local history or details of the former occupants or of the building itself? How much of this is just hearsay and how much actual authentic knowledge? This information could well colour the witness's mental approach and even create an atmosphere in which imagination can take command. It could unfortunately also make the witness provide untrue details of his own experience in an attempt to fit in with the known facts.

The attitude of friends and neighbours will almost certainly cause the original story to be modified, added to for effect, or treated as a joke. When the interviewer arrives it may then be difficult to assess what in the mind of the witness is true and what is fictional "colouring". One must, however, with tact and diplomacy, attempt to sort out the wheat from the chaff.

In cases of poltergeist activity in Council property it should be remembered that there is a possibility that the events have been exaggerated in order to obtain more suitable accommodation. It is not unknown for a family to make use of normal incidents, reporting that they were due to the ghost and fraudulently attempting to duplicate genuine phenomena.

More often than not these attempts are pitifully obvious, but to the new researcher the statements made and descriptions given may sound genuine. There have also been one or two incidents where neighbours having seen the publicity and attraction caused by the "poltergeist", decided that it was rather fun to be haunted, and reported they too had a ghost. If this sort of situation is not nipped in the bud straight away there is no knowing where it will end. One recalls the Witches of Salem, and the mass hysteria which gripped the locality for years before common sense finally prevailed. Unfortunately a mixture of genuine and fraudulent phenomena can never be ruled out in such cases and it is only through questioning that one may arrive at some conclusion.

Enquire as to the sort of books that are read and the type of films and television programmes that are most favoured and enjoyed. A deep interest in psychic matters, witchcraft and similar subjects might indicate a case of deliberate or semi-deliberate fraud, or at least a hoax, although it may well merely suggest a genuine interest in the subject,

If you are interested in a poltergeist case, then obviously you should meet the probable cause of the trouble. It should be remembered that where, as in most cases, an adolescent is acting as the "agent" the boy or girl in question may well be found to be mentally unstable, or even suffering from some physical defect.

In many cases the household involved can be classified as "under-privileged", and it is often because of the general environment that the child is driven to create disturbances which will eventually spotlight attention on the phenomena unconsciously started. Realising s/he is able by some means to "control" the phenomena, the child increases the strength, variety, and number of incidents until the parents are terrified by the activity and appeal to the Council to be rehoused, not realising (or flatly refusing to believe) that the cause lies with their own offspring.

But as one investigator said "Begun in fun, continued in fraud and closed in fright": the child becomes scared by the attitude of his/her parents, and eventually the phenomena cease. In serious cases the child's mental stability can be affected, and the result can even be what is commonly known as "split personality". The youngster, realising the distress that is caused, is on the one hand inclined to dissociate himself from the disturbances, while on the other hand he continues to produce the phenomena and enjoys the publicity which results.

When talking to the child, therefore, be gentle, relaxed and friendly. Should any phenomena occur at the time, don't be disturbed but try, though it might may not be easy at first, to ignore the occurrence. Encourage the child to share this relaxed feeling and attempt to impart this atmosphere to the parents. Dissuade the people concerned from any action which could attract attention from the press, for such an action is quite likely to worsen the situation. What is required is a fuller understanding of the child and a more peaceful existence for the victims. Once they understand the problem half the worry is alleviated.

If the phenomena appear to be of a poltergeist nature, but there is no child involved, it may be that the trouble is being created by the youngest member of the family, if s/he has an underlying motive. I suggested earlier that one should find out whether the household consisted of a closely knit family unit. If there is any discord it may be caused by animosity felt towards one individual, and it may be that the agent of the poltergeist phenomena is hoping in some way to cause the object of his/her dislike to go away. This is one reason why questioning any child in the household could prove useful – but never suggest to the child that there is someone he does not like. Auto-suggestion is a powerful boost to a young undeveloped mind.

If there appear to be no children on the premises, ask where they are and if it would be possible to meet them later. Council house tenants almost invariably have to be parents in order to qualify for accommodation.

"Phenomena" created as a joke, by deliberate fraud, as a hoax, or just "ghosting for a giggle" is still prevalent, and is sometimes produced with great effect. As more teenagers have less to occupy their brains and hands, some of the more imaginative will turn to scaring people by concocting the most elaborate "phantoms".

Never show annoyance if, after a few minutes of questioning, the witness admits that the incident was imagined or that he only told the reporter "for a laugh". It may of course also be some time before the perpetrator of the hoax is prepared to acknowledge that he was responsible. Point out the consequences of any repeat performance. Mention the fact that in serious cases the police have taken action, especially where a witness with a weak heart has been affected.

Having questioned the witness as thoroughly as possible, you should then discuss the desirability of investigating the matter in depth, and arrange to return with your equipment. Naturally this should be shortly before the same time of the day at which the initial incident occurred and, if possible, on the same day of the week or month. If the phenomena occurred, for example, at 7.30 pm, then you should have everything set up by at least 7 pm. The occupant should be encouraged to take a detached view of your activities. An explanation of each piece of apparatus and its use will help to attain this aim.

Firstly, examine the inside of the premises thoroughly. Open all cupboards, be sure to visit any cellars, and look for faults in the floor, walls and roof. Note any recent repairs carried out to the structure, and of course take measurements; it has already been pointed out that discrepancies between outer and inner wall thicknesses could be accounted for by secret tunnels, walled-up cupboards, priest's holes, papered-over apertures, etc – behind or inside which many things could be concealed. Photograph as many unusual features as possible, or make sketches giving dimensions.

When moving from room to room close each cupboard door, check the locks and seal the room with self-adhesive tape on the doorframe – not all round the doorway, but with a short length at some inconspicuous spot. It might be worthwhile using coloured tape, as the transparent variety is likely to be found in almost every household. Seal up the windows in a similar way. I would suggest that some means of identification, other than the colour, be used to ensure that a possible hoaxer doesn't fake your seal. This could be a slip of paper with your signature on it, stuck to the inner side of the tape so that it is hidden from view.

In the room or area affected by the haunting or poltergeist activity take photographs of the whole room, each wall from floor to ceiling, windows, the ceiling itself, and several views of the contents, to record the position of each piece of furniture. If you wish to be super-efficient you could wire up contact switches under everything so that a light or bell operates when the object is moved, but a simpler method, adopted by many investigators, is merely to circle items with chalk.

To help eliminate the possibility of fraud, the occupants of the premises should be asked to stay in one room while you are carrying out your preliminary work. (This room should not of course be the affected area.)

Tape-recording apparatus, time-operated cameras, monitor television sets, detectors to record capacitance changes, and minimum/maximum thermometers should then be set up inside the haunted room, and a photograph taken of the equipment on site with a plan showing its exact position.

I should point out here that this sort of procedure is recommended only for poltergeist cases, or for those which seem to offer good evidence for a genuine repeated haunting which has occurred recently, and not one of which there has been no report for some years.

If phenomena occur while you are on the premises, you can only hope that you are in the vicinity at the time and have kept a close watch on any individual suspected of being the cause. This situation demonstrates the desirability of having a companion with you, not only to assist in setting up the equipment, but to keep a check on the activities of members of the household. Evidence from two people is better than one person's report, and evidence from a group is better still.

In a case where the building is empty, it is strongly recommended that there should be more than one investigator involved. And they should preferably keep together so that they can substantiate the other's experience. Ideally a group should be involved under such circumstances, and searches and activities should be carried out in pairs. It is not unknown for one individual, new to the complexities of carrying out a thorough investigation, to return home without telling any of the others. Reasons vary – boredom and fright are the most common.

Once the equipment is set up all you can do is wait and see, but do check through the premises and apparatus fairly frequently.

CHAPTER 9

Confirmatory Evidence

Do you accept everything anyone tells you? Do you believe everything you read in the papers or see on television? Sixty years ago there were many, who after Richard Dimbleby's broadcast in 1957 on the first of April, accepted that if they visit an area of Italy or Switzerland they will find the spaghetti trees featured on the television programme. There are even more who are happy to believe various stories about haggis hunting in Scotland.

Some of these believers have no means of checking the statements they believe without visiting the countries concerned, and some don't want to. But if you, who are on the site of phenomena, wish to establish and corroborate information given you, then you must obtain confirmatory evidence. Corroboratory evidence is that which independently supports or confirms other evidence obtained.

This can be achieved by several methods. One of the best is to interview other witnesses of the phenomena, whose names and addresses should be obtained when discussing the matter with the initial contact. You will have gained an impression as to their honesty, their imaginative powers, their inventiveness or their integrity, and will have to decide the value, or otherwise, of pursuing the case.

Is the second witness a relative of the person just interviewed, or are they close friends? Obviously such a relationship could affect the authenticity of any statement. Did the second witness see or experience the phenomena at the same time and in the same place? If so, does the description exactly match that given in the initial report? Before accepting this as genuine, refer to fig 4 again and remember that it is possible, depending where the second witness was standing, that he should *not* have seen the apparition in exactly the same way. If he claims that he did, and from his position at the time this would appear impossible, the explanation could either be a telepathic link through the original witness, or plain imagination in an attempt to please you and support his companion's story.

Questioning other witnesses is naturally carried out in the same fashion as in the case of the first witness, but information as to the nature and character of the individual who reported the incident can, with tact, also be obtained. It could also be interesting to ascertain the reason why the second witness and any other person involved failed to report the incident in the first place.

The answer could be valuable in assessing the whole case. It should be pointed out that it is advisable to examine any supporting witness in his own home, or at least out of earshot of the original informant.

Where there are no other witnesses to the phenomena, you should obtain some form of character witness, unless the impression gained at the initial interview is entirely satisfactory. But this sort of action really depends on how deeply you wish to become involved and how thorough you require your report to be.

How strong a character is the supporting individual? It could be that he was in fact directly responsible for the experience. Auto-suggestion combined with imagination in a highly-strung individual has been known to cause a ghost to be seen.

Don't dismiss the case because the friend or associate is unable to corroborate the initial report. There could be a variety of reasons to account for this attitude. Jealously of the publicity given to the original witness, a change of mind, or anxiety due to lack of understanding, are all possible causes of such a situation. Should the second witness be practically a stranger to the first, find out how the two became associated. For example, a builder employed by a lady trying to obtain some publicity for her newly-opened restaurant by reporting that she had seen an apparition could well be in a situation where he felt it desirable, even though not truthful, to confirm his employer's statement.

There are many instances, of course, where the original witness does not even know the phenomenon has been experienced by others. It is for this reason that one needs to examine the past history of the premises. Confirmation of dates given by the witness, of building, of alternations to the structure, of deaths and burials, all help to authenticate the report. All this type of information can be obtained from sources already mentioned: church records, libraries and museums.

Never be surprised if the description given by the other witness does not correspond exactly with that already noted down. Various people see various things. A short person will possibly say that a person of average height is "tall", and vice versa. A woman will probably make a mental note of the clothing of an apparition if it is seen for a long enough period, whereas a man may notice features rather than dress. It may therefore be helpful to ask whether it was as tall "as that bush", or some other object whose height can be assessed and try to establish the overall colour – white, grey, black or what?

There is a possibility of course that the corroborating witness saw something in addition to what was seen by the first interviewee. More detail may be provided of the apparition and the phenomena, or even another apparition may be described. One case involved five witnesses, three of whom saw the phantom of a man, while the others saw ghosts of a man or woman – all at an identical time in the same location.

If the second witness describes the phenomena that appear to be completely unrelated to the original report, you should check back after obtaining the maximum amount of detail, with the initial witness, to find out whether he remembers seeing "anything else".

When you meet the corroborating witness for the first time, never give any information which might cause him/her to create a description matching the one already obtained. Merely ask if s/he experienced or saw anything "at the same time" as your informant. Then, of course, check with him/her exactly what time that was. If he requests details of what your informant claims to have seen" I would suggest that you dodge the question by replying, "I am more interested in learning what *you have experienced.*" Even if the questioner pursues the matter, never provide a description. It may even be better to fabricate a little by saying for example, "Mrs Jones thought she saw something near the High Street but thought you could help me with a more detailed description." The apparition in this instance would not have been seen actually in the High Street but in its locality, and putting a reply in this fashion could obtain confirmation of the exact location. Consider also if any identification may have been influenced by other sources, including any previous coverage in the media or on the internet.

One must assess not only the gullibility of other witnesses, but also their own character. Unfortunately, in some cases, more often than not poltergeist incidents, the only other witnesses are children, one of whom may well be the agent. Although you should attempt to question them, it will probably be difficult to do so away from parents, and considerable diplomacy may be called for. Parents are always liable to speak for their children and constantly interrupt the examination of them but parental wishes naturally have to prevail.

Too often one experiences the kind of situation in which a fond mother will say something like "Oh yes, I saw the ghost didn't I Peter?" What is the poor lad to say but "Yes," – how does he know if she didn't see it? At other times parents become too protective and are reluctant to allow any questioning of their offspring, even though they may be the only other witnesses to an interesting incident. If gentle persuasion fails to assist, you could imply that your investigations will be worthless without further information from the other witnesses. (Should the reply be "so what?" then all you can do is to leave with as much politeness as possible, but fortunately this seldom happens). The child should be asked to provide in their own words an account of their experience, providing that revisiting it does not cause distress. This opportunity for the child to speak freely should be viewed as the core of the interview and the most reliable source of accurate information. During this phase, the interviewer's role should be that of a facilitator, not an interrogator. Tact and patience should be used specially with children, and you should be especially careful not to suggest or imply answers, since the testimony of children may be more easily shaped and distorted than with many adults.

Should the initial report have been gleaned from the local press, it might be worthwhile to have a chat with the reporter who covered the story. Most local journalists I find are extremely astute and helpful. They can probably assist you with some background knowledge (which often has not appeared in the press) and their own views, in confidence (and please respect it), on the particular case involved may well be of considerable assistance.

Corroborative statements alone, of course, are not enough to authenticate a case of phenomena. During the nineteen-sixties, in the offices of a motoring school at Maidstone, the manager persistently heard the sound over a period of two years of footsteps, "coming from upstairs". The report stated the three floors above the ground floor office in the old, rather dilapidated, premises were unused, and the stairs led nowhere in particular except to "empty cupboards and serving hatches." It was impossible for anyone to enter the rooms except through the office, the windows of which were heavily barred.

The assistant manager confirmed that he too had heard the noises; unlike his superior he was not afraid of them, although he was unable to offer any rational explanation for the phenomenon. At this stage the incidents could have been accepted as genuine hauntings. Early records indicated that previous tenants had heard the footsteps; the building, originally a private house, had accommodated many families during its existence; there appeared to be no reason to assume that the close proximity of the river could be associated with the sounds, and the two interviewed executives were convinced that they had heard the footsteps.

When the manager retired and the assistant was promoted to replace him, the younger man was determined to "get to the bottom of it", and spent many hours examining the whole of the property. When at one stage he heard noises which resembled those of furniture being moved, he realised that the solution to the "phantom footsteps" would be found in the adjoining building – a hotel. On enquiring from the manager he learnt that many years previously the building containing the offices of the motoring school had formed part of the hotel, but it was reduced in size by partitioning off some of the original premises. The result was that one of the main staircases was split into two sections, one of the office building and the other remaining in the hotel.

The result was obvious. Because the walls were so insubstantial, whenever a guest or member of staff walked up the stairs in the hotel it sounded as if they were in the other building. Not surprising really, for they were using the same stair treads.

When the case involves phenomena in a Council house or social housing, making contact with the authorities is recommended. Unfortunately, it may take some time to contact the individual officer responsible for the particular property. Even then a council official is likely to prove unwilling to discuss the matter in any great detail, despite assurances from the researcher that he is not the press, nor representing a consumer body, and not trying to obtain alternative accommodation for the tenants. If you are fortunate you may gain some interesting insights into the phenomena and the tenants from a sympathetic Council employee, but again any information must be treated as confidential, and should only be used to assess the authenticity of the case.

If the original witness is a child and you have to rely on confirmation of the story from the parents, there is a strong possibility that the adults will embellish the story, or attempt to get the child to invent details, in order to match some known incident or the description of some deceased relative or friend. One can only make certain, under these circumstances, that every minute detail of the child's own statement is taken down and every comment or suggestion made by the parents is clearly marked as such.

Where there is only one witness and no history of previous haunting or any immediately apparent explanation for the phenomena, an attempt should be made, having obtained the necessary permission to duplicate the incident. One case where this could have been done, probably with positive results, occurred in a print shop in Cambridgeshire. A teenage machine minder, working overtime alone in the basement at about 6.30 p.m. one January evening saw immediately above a flight of steps, "a large white cloud." Terrified, he jumped behind his machine, and as he looked towards the shape, "it started to move across the room. It was a white mass with a grey mass in the middle and I gradually saw that it was shaped like a human body…I was scared and flew out the door."

Now some Litho printing machines puff jets of powdered chalk on to the sheets of paper as they come away from the printing roller, to facilitate drying and preventing sticking. If there was some fault in the machine a cloud of powdered chalk could easily be created. The draught from the stairway would hold the cloud for some seconds before it moved back to the printing machine, drawn by the constant movement of the wheels and paper.

It is believed the lad knew the story of a man who had been crushed to death at the foot of the stairs when the building was used as a brewery, and on a cold, probably silent, night his imagination under such conditions could easily have created the "ghost". Any shape that at all resembles the human outline, however vague, is immediately assumed to be that of an apparition.

At least four people have witnessed apparitions and experienced phenomena at Kirkstall Abbey House Museum, Leeds between 1968-73, and Leonard Cooper, a Yorkshire author whose grandfather lived in the house before it became a museum states that ghosts were known to exist there as long ago as the 1880s. In this sort of case it would strengthen any report to have statements from as many witnesses as possible, provided of course that the majority at least were of a sound character and had described their experiences without knowing the details of the phenomena witnessed by others. Unfortunately, as pointed out earlier, once an incident has been reported in the local paper the witnesses' stories become exaggerated.

What could be regarded as an ideal case of a haunting occurred in Sussex in 1967. Four workmen were employed on renovating a house. Two of them stated that one evening in March they saw an old woman walk up the pathway and tell them that they had "done enough" and that they were to stop. "Having done this she turned and walked a few steps only to vanish when nearing a corner of the site". Both men gave independent statements as to the phantom's appearance, and a third, working in an upstairs room confirmed their stories by stating that he too had seen the apparition, though naturally he had heard nothing. On following up the tale it was realised that the three descriptions given by the men were identical, and tallied exactly with that of a former owner of the house who had died some two years earlier.

As to the command to stop work, I can only offer the theory that it could very well have been given to a gardener at the time the apparition was created. In common with other such "spoken messages" it would have been received by the workmen purely through the mind's ear, and not as a truly verbal comment.

Should your own home be haunted and you are considering employing workmen to renovate it or carry out some structural alterations, don't ever tell them the house has a ghost: the work may cost you more money if you do. A team if builders working on a house in Bramley, Yorkshire, in 1970, demanded more money because of a ghost. The plasterer complained that he heard the sounds of chains rattling and human moaning, a bricklayer followed suit and began to hear the same phenomena; finally the whole group were so frightened that they threatened to walk off the site unless an immediate increase in their rates of pay was agreed. Or so at least it was reported. One wonders if the Union involved would have seriously considered making a strike "official" on the grounds of "Psychic phenomena."

In cases of animal ghosts it is rather more difficult to assess the validity of confirming witnesses, a "white horse" is a white horse to anyone, a "black cat" is a black cat. One can only hope that evidence of a documentary nature can provide confirmation.

At Ascot in 1968 four out of six demolition workers claimed that they had seen the apparition of a white horse while demolishing stables of the former Royal Ascot Hotel. To obtain evidence for the existence of such an animal at one time would call for considerable patience in tracing the last owner, or (since he may no longer be alive) relatives and friends who might know of the creatures kept there and if one particular steed was the favourite. One would then require to know if it were dead and, if so, whether it was destroyed, and how and when it died. Because there may have been several animals who matched the description this sort of case could well be a complete waste of time (save as an exercise in persistence).

The ghost of an unseen cat is supposed to haunt The Old Nag's Head at Holme Hale in Norfolk. The owner is reported to have said "It can often be felt jumping on to beds and curling up for sleep." It is usually hardly worthwhile pursuing this kind of case, for even the most enthusiastic ghost hunter would probably be inclined to move on to a case which offers greater potential and challenge.

Hotels are premises where confirmatory evidence should be comparatively easy to obtain, and few guests know all the historical details of the inn they are staying at. The addresses of hotels are usually freely available, and stories of ghosts and hauntings are seldom repeated by landlords for fear of affecting future businesses.

One hotel reported in the *Peterborough Evening Telegraph* to be haunted, and included in Jack Hallam's *The Haunted Inns of England* (Wolfe) is the Talbot at Oundle in Northamptonshire. Room 5 seems affected by weird noises and spells of sudden cold, and a cook, employed there for twenty-two years, saw the apparition of a woman in a long dress with a small cap and apron.

A case of psychical phenomena of an unusual type in another hotel sounds rather like childish pranks, but might bear further enquiry. The proprietress of the building, the Lowyber Manor Hotel in Alston, Cumberland, told the *Cumberland News* in August 1972 that soon after she arrived four years ago, she found black coal marks on bedroom doors in a house which has no open fires. Footsteps have been heard on floors covered with carpet, and "more recently the lavatory has been heard to flush itself during the night". Local legend claims that a girl was burned in a fire in a building on the site over 100 years ago.

A series of unusual and inexplicable incidents occurred at the Punchbowl Hotel in Sefton, near Liverpool, during 1971; many of them could be corroborated by witnesses, but whether any factual history concerning them can be ascertained is another matter. The barmaid and the landlord's daughter saw a ghost of a man twice in two weeks when the hotel was closed. According to the *Liverpool Echo* three customers filled in their joint football pools coupon in the haunted room, experienced a "premonition that they would win", and received a cheque for £90 000. Unfortunately for the promoters, photographs taken of the winners in the room failed to register anything unusual.

All sorts of things seem to happen at Sefton, for a local gravedigger received assistance from a ghost, "stripped to the waist" according to a witness, in digging a grave. The workman himself was unable to see the apparition but could confirm that more soil had been removed than he had dug up.

One of the frustrating aspects of some phenomena is that the story can never be checked, clarified or confirmed. A couple known to me, who live near Guildford, were on holiday in Devon in 1955, touring the area of Paignton with the intention of recording church inns. On passing one situated at a cross-roads they made a mental note of it, intending to return the following day after keeping their appointment. They described the building and the clothes that the customers wore, for they were "gathered round the entrance laughing and joking, the women with baskets and mugs of beer." When they returned to the site the next day all they found was an open field.

Despite exhaustive enquiries from the police, the local library, the museum, the archaeological society, the Council and the press, there is nothing to record that an inn was ever on the site, and no film-making was in progress in the area.

For this sort of incident there never can be any satisfactory explanation, not even that of plain imagination. "Mistaken locality" will not begin to answer this particular case. The couple had stopped their car a few feet from the cross-roads, and to ensure that they would be able to recognise the place again they drew a sketch plan of it. The town clerk, to whom I wrote, was able to recognise the site from that hastily drawn plan nearly twenty years later. The gentleman concerned is a qualified engineer and hardly likely to dream up a story like this to no purpose, and his wife is a senior Civil Servant.

Another tale which may sound even more incredible is that of the wooden floor of a shed which was completed overnight at Woolmer Green in Hertfordshire. How and by what has never been established. Is it possible that psychokinesis is the answer? The owner certainly wanted the job finished quickly.

You will have realised that seeing another witness may give rise to fresh problems; but it is also possible that the same form of questioning as that used in the initial instance may lead to your hearing of other hauntings which warrant investigation. I am referring to the possibility that the second person interviewed may have a greater knowledge of the locality and provide leads to other sites. However, do not be tempted to chase off after another haunting in the middle of an investigation, unless it is absolutely essential to be the first on the spot. Usually changing course in this way will only confuse you and the individuals concerned. Just make notes of as much detail as possible and continue with the original enquiries.

Even if you are relying on a tape-recorder when obtaining information, always take a notebook as well. Machines have been known to break down in the middle of a conversation or even fail to record anything at all. It can also be highly annoying for the witness if, when he is in the middle of providing a detailed description of an apparition, the investigator has to say "Excuse me a moment, I'll have to change cassettes/batteries. This one has run out."

So be prepared for any eventuality.

CHAPTER 10

Description of phenomena

As part of the examination of the witness, during the interview you must naturally obtain a full description of the incident or apparition, and ascertain the period of time over which it was seen or experienced. If the witness is vague on this last point, ask him to visualise the incident again while you count out seconds, for few people realise when stating that they "saw it for a couple of minutes" that a minute is a comparatively long time: in fact, few ghosts have been visible for more than thirty seconds.

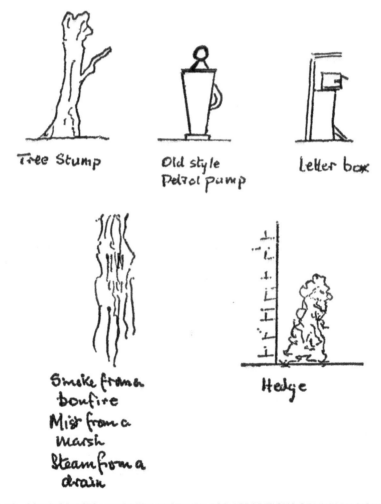

Tree Stump

Old style Petrol pump

Letter box

Smoke from a bonfire
Mist from a marsh
Steam from a drain

Hedge

Fig. 12 - SOME OBJECTS HAVE BEEN MISTAKEN FOR APPARITIONS OF HUMAN FIGURES

Check with the person involved that the figure really *did* resemble a human, for one needs more than "a tall triangular shape with two black spots for eyes" or "a white mist in the shape of a woman" to accept that the phenomenon actually was an apparition. Even old-style petrol pumps seen on a misty evening may be mistaken for human figures. A letter-box on the side of the road a few yards from my house has often been mistaken by motorists, when speeding round the corner at night, for the figure of a man. Other "human shapes" are shown in figs. 12 and 13. This problem of interpretation often arises with anomalous images in photographs where imagination and a subconscious tendency to visualise patterns may lead people to misidentify or imagine a shape or marking to be a ghostly presence.

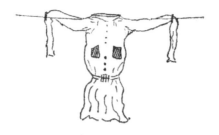

Fig. 13

One 'phantom' was reported four times before being established as a dress on a washing line. Grey in colour and seen late at night and only in a car's headlights several feet away, it terrified several people for some time.

"What were the clothes of the apparition like in style and colouring?" This type of question may produce a hasty sketch of the figure if you are lucky. If this is sufficiently detailed it may be possible to establish the period involved, though many witnesses will give their own interpretations as to styles and fashions: "old" can mean anything from medieval to Edwardian, and assessments will also depend partly on the age of the witness.

Should the description seem to indicate, say, an early Victorian style, while the building involved was constructed in the 1970s, this would strongly suggest that an earlier building formerly occupied the site, or if not a building then something with human connections. This could be as simple as a tree, a pond or a seat. Or it could alternatively suggest that the witness was mistaken and had simply seen a teenager in "trendy" clothes, some of which bear a strong resemblance to 19th century styles.

Did the door *really* open? Did the witness have to close it physically afterwards? There are not many phenomenal incidents involving doors where a "ghost opened it" *without closing it again*. In other words, it never did physically move. The movement was part of the hallucination, and thus tapes or cotton fixed across a doorway would remain unbroken despite the witness having 'seen' the door open. An automatic camera shot would only register a closed door, though it might possibly record an image and a "phantom open door" at the same time.

Was there a mirror near or in line with the site of the "phantom"? Could it be seen in the glass? What time of day did the ghost make its appearance, and what time of year? If the figure was "a misty shadow", probably seen outside, where are the nearest ventilating shaft covers to drains and sewers? Did the apparition move and, if so quickly, slowly, in a jerking fashion, or did it just glide? Were the feet visible and, if so, were they on the ground?

As I said earlier, don't suggest answers, and don't ever emphasise a particular word when putting a question. This is an old stage trick and can be shown to work if one asks "Was it white, black, or grey?" The positive answer is "black", but indecisive introverts may give either of the other two colours; the question to put should merely be "What colour was it?" or "Did you notice any colouring?" (If the answer is "black" or "grey", and the figure was seen at night in a darkened room, or an unlit street, there will be obvious difficulties in accepting information, which may well be offered at the same time, such as that "it had dark brown eyes, I could see them quite clearly").

Some investigators have suggested that there has been a decline in detailed, well-witnessed apparition reports since the 19th century, matched by an increasing vagueness in apparitional forms themselves, with less distinct apparitions and more reports of shadows and hazes.[38]

In cases of noise phenomena all one can hope for is a better description than "footsteps". Were they heavy, regular or light; did they sound like running, creeping or shuffling? Were they definitely human, or did they resemble an animal's padding steps? Where did they start from and finish? Where is the nearest heating unit, chimney breast, radiator, night storage heater unit to the starting point? Are the floor boards placed north/south, east/west, or

---

[38] Hallson, Peter, (1986) Correspondence, *Journal of the Society for Psychical Research* Vol. 53, No. 803 331-332.

mixed? When was the floor last examined or treated for woodrot or beetle? Has an air brick been replaced recently? Regular gusts of wind through air vents below flooring level can cause noises similar to footsteps. If the sounds stopped at some particular spot, what might here be at the end of the walk? A cupboard? A sealed doorway? When was it constructed?

This chapter seems to consist of a great many questions, but it is from these that one can glean valuable data; and in order to lay down general guidelines it is necessary to try to cater for every possible eventuality.

Tapping noises vary from sounds like a woodpecker to gentle metallic raps probably caused through "water-hammer" and/or recent installation of a central heating system. Because sounds are often difficult to describe, you may be tempted to try to duplicate them in order to identify their basic structure, and it can sometimes be difficult not to suggest sources to the witness. If you do make exploratory taps and are using a tape recorder, be sure to introduce yourself by saying something like, "I'm going to rap this piece of wood three times. Could you tell me if the noise you heard sounded like this?" If this precaution is not taken, when you play the recording back hours, or even days later, you may well have forgotten how many times you tried to duplicate the noise, and find that you have recorded or think you have recorded an additional sound.

Intermediate smells are another sensation difficult to put into words: the witness may compare the odour to "a dustbin", "sewage", or "perfume" – the latter being extremely hard to define. A lady in Mountfield, Sussex, told me that an old oak beam in her cottage emitted the fragrance of "a sweet perfume" at certain times, but was naturally unable to name it. Without any clue it was impossible to guess at the source; also the sensitivity of individuals' sense of smell vary. What is "sweet" or "musky" to one person may be "sickly" or "mousy" to another.

Just to add to your difficulties, colour definition also varies, and real problems arise when trying to obtain descriptions from someone suffering from colour-blindness. In these instances you can only hope for more detail from other witnesses, or try using comparisons to establish what exactly is meant.

Returning to a question mentioned earlier, what made the witness think the incident was paranormal? Did the "ghost" act in a peculiar way and, if so, how? Was it just dressed in old-fashioned clothes but otherwise behaved normally? Were the sounds heard of a type never experienced before? If the witness had previous experience of psychic phenomena, did this last incident resemble it in any way? If so, were the circumstances surrounding the occurrence similar in any way?

Some people when talking about the phenomena experienced are inclined to bring irrelevancies into the story, but do not ignore them or try to stop the flow. What may appear to have nothing to do with the case could provide an insight into the person's mental state at the time or it could indicate exaggeration. You will have plenty of time later to sort out the wheat from the chaff.

Should the witness already have written a statement describing his/her experience then a lot of your work will already have been done, but this action will be unusual. Some investigators ask the witness to write out the statement him/herself and then sign it. I feel that this may cause the omission of a lot of valuable background material, and as one would have to question the witness afterwards in any case it would probably not be much use except to stress the serious nature of the investigation.

Descriptions included in statements usually need clarifying, and during the interview which follows they are often contradicted, amended or modified. The witness could be asked to amend the statement and sign the correction, which would further emphasise that s/he alone is responsible for what s/he has said. This action itself is inclined to deter imaginative and fraudulent comments, but by the time an interview is concluded the papers may well have become so corrected that re-writing would be needed – something few people would be agreeable to, especially if it is a long report.

You could offer to get the statement typed and come back for the witness to sign it later, but in doing so you are risking a refusal, the witness having been "got at" by relatives or the press in the meantime. A refusal could mean that the whole case was imagined. If you point out that others will treat the refusal as significant, the witness may then agree to sign the paper. Personally, to record the witnesses' answers and comments seems to me to be a more satisfactory procedure. If necessary you can then type the statement and submit it for signature.

The same procedure would be adopted in the case of the second witness, or the person to whom the story was initially told. The first person who heard the story is, of course, quite a valuable link in the chain, and you will probably not be lucky enough to be that person. This individual should be regarded as the source of a vital part of the corroborating evidence. His/her statement can be nearly as important as the initial report, especially if the tale is related a large number of times, gathering more embellishments at each telling.

Having noted the description of an apparition you should enquire as to whether it matches that of anyone the eye-witness knows or knew.

Examine closely the circumstances of the identification; for how long was the figure visible, how far away, in what light, was observation impeded, had the witness seen the person before and if so how often? If only seen occasionally, had the witness any special reason for remembering the person? Recognition of a relative may be more reliable than that of a comparative stranger, but it should be remembered that mistakes in recognising close friends and relatives are sometimes made in daily life, and there may be far more scope for mistakes if a witness wishes to see the dead person.

It may be worth obtaining a picture of the person if they were known and seeing if there is any material discrepancy between the witness's description and the appearance in the photograph (allowing for age and circumstances when the photograph was taken). The possibility that a person may have seen an image of the person before may have to be considered; this is a problem for all situations where eye-witness identification is used, because of the proliferation of photographs of people on social media sites and the internet.

Analogous principles apply with voice recognition, which is altogether more difficult than any visual identification. The amount of time a person spent with the person in life will be relevant to assessing the likely accuracy of any such identification of an audio recording when dealing with Electronic Voice Phenomena.

Thus you can establish whether it can truly be classified as an apparition of the dead or a haunting apparition. Remember that if a witness recognised the phantom and knew that it was someone dead the case cannot be correctly treated as genuine beyond all doubt.

A list of potential questions is included in Appendix One.

CHAPTER 11

Conclusions and the future

By now the investigator will be nearing the final stages of compiling his/her report, assessing the evidence and reaching a conclusion as to the authenticity of the phenomena. But before taking any action, re-examine the report in depth and check that the many questions raised have been answered to your complete satisfaction. Documentary and photographic evidence should be comprehensive, but be prepared to accept advice, comment and fair criticism, for it is only by this means that you can hope to learn exactly what is required to authenticate a haunting.

Where incidents are continual it may be advisable to submit an interim report, provided that this is sufficiently detailed to stress the need for continuing the investigation.

It is wise, if this is your intention, to request the full co-operation of the witnesses, or "victims" in maintaining a close record of incidents, by noting times and exact locations of the phenomena as well as the locality of other people in the household at the time. Continuity can thus be assured; but although you may expect that the witness will probably advise you of further phenomena, never rely on this assistance. Assure your informant, however, that any costs incurred (such as postage or telephone calls) will be met.

If the disturbances continue to frighten the occupiers of the affected property, several courses are open to you. The people concerned may well request, even beg, you to "get rid of the ghost". In certain circumstances it may be thought advisable to inform them tactfully of your own findings and theories especially if the case is of poltergeist activity. Point out that incidents will gradually fade away as the agent gets older, and meanwhile they should try to ignore the activity and play down the whole matter. To express a greater personal interest in the agent him/herself often hastens the ending of the phenomena, but to publicise the incidents and to make it obvious that one is affected by them may cause an increase in the strength and frequency of the incidents.

One such case was in Essex, where a fourteen-year-old boy was the agent of poltergeist activity; as the phenomena increased in intensity, as a result of the attention paid to the occurrences, the youngster became more unmanageable. In desperation the parents took the boy, accompanied by an uncle and another relative, to the local church where a special service had been arranged by the vicar. So intense was the power that during the course of the special service the vicar collapsed at the altar and the boy "went berserk". It will be realised that the youngster was enjoying being the centre of attention, and strongly antagonistic towards the church or anything else, for that matter which might have restricted his performance and deprived him of attention that was being paid to him.

He eventually broke free from his guardians and ran back to his school where he attempted to set it alight. I understand both he and the priest had to undergo considerable psychiatric treatment before they were able to return to normal. The phenomena eventually ceased and the youngster was later happily employed, I believe, in an engineering firm.

The action to take where a poltergeist case is concerned is firstly to examine the religious outlook of the individuals and to ascertain their attitude towards methods of eradicating the trouble. Having explained the probability that one person in the household is responsible, albeit unconsciously, for the trouble, suggest that the local doctor be consulted. He may well recommend a course of tranquillizers for a short period.

If this suggestion is not acceptable, find out whether the witness would object to a medium being called in to assist. As pointed out earlier, a medium may not necessarily be a Spiritualist, so it is advisable to check views on this form of religion before arranging such action. A medium will probably feel it necessary to go into a trance in order to contact the "entity", and this action should be explained to the victim. It should be pointed out here, that once definite action has been called for or arranged, it is often found that the phenomena will cease automatically – providing a further demonstration of the psychological or psychosomatic aspect of the poltergeist phenomena.

If the individuals concerned are avowed Christians, then a visit from the local vicar may be of value. Really it is a question of what "theatricals" or ritual will be acceptable to the culprit's subconscious, or, in the case of apparitions to the witness's mind. If the performance satisfies the needs for strong, awesome ceremony, then there is a fair chance that it will be successful in eradicating, not the phenomena itself, but the experience of the witness concerned. All you are really attempting to achieve is a "mental blanket" – just as parents are trying to do when they tell their children "not to imagine things".

In desperation some people call for exorcism, without realising exactly what is involved, and because "exorcism can be and has been carried out by any Christian and even non-Christians in the name of Christ" it will perhaps be useful to quote from a work such as *Deliverance: Psychic Disturbances and Occult Involvement* (1996, 2012) edited by Michael Perry and published by the Society for the Promotion of Christian Knowledge.[39] Less than one fifth of this book is taken up with possession and exorcism. The term preferred today is deliverance ministry rather than the ministry of exorcism, the Church seeing its role as a much wider pastoral one, rather than focusing on specific rites and rituals.

Since the 1970s the Anglican Church has updated its views on ministering to those who believe they are troubled by hauntings or psychic phenomena of any kind. As the Guide recognises many parish priests feel 'out of their depth' because they have no previous experiences of such cases, but the church provides help and resources which encourage priests to assist people with these. It has been realised that in practice counselling and psychological support as much as any prayer or ritual is often what people afflicted by a haunting require, and it is recognised that many cases have a purely psychological origin or have a natural explanation. The Church of England may be called upon to assist people who have dabbled in occult practices or scared themselves playing with Ouija boards or indulged in other psychic pursuits in a light hearted-manner. Many of these problems may be resolved with the application of common sense and reason, sometimes using simple blessings or prayers. The need for a psychotherapeutic and counselling approach is recognised with respect to poltergeist activity along with the acceptance that exorcism may be wholly ineffective with certain classes of phenomena that are devoid of any spiritual content. As with parapsychology, the responsible approach is emphasised; it is necessary to differentiate between facts and interpretation. Those suffering from psychotic illnesses, neurotic disorders, bereavement reactions, psychological damage from spiritual or quasi-spiritual practices and incidents of spontaneous PK do not need exorcisms. This is particularly so with what appear to be recording-type apparitions which have no consciousness.

Great care is taken within the Church of England and within the Roman Catholic Church in Britain in approaching the topic of exorcism because of the sensational headlines the subject can attract and, more significantly, the

---

[39] Perry, Michael (1996, 2012) *Deliverance: Psychic Disturbances and Occult Involvement.* UK.Society for the Promotion of Christian Knowledge.

acknowledgement that it can cause more harm than good in many cases involving vulnerable persons. The guide book *Deliverance* recognises that reckless talk of exorcism and casting out demons and devils can often have a traumatic and highly damaging effect upon already nervous and suggestible individuals, as can involvement with certain Charismatic, New Age and occult practices and cults. For similar reasons, the broadcasting regulator controls what may be transmitted on television concerning the practice of exorcism because of the disproportionate effect it may have on vulnerable people. For such reasons a ghost hunter should never attempt to perform such a ritual or rite, or even pretend to do so.

Exorcism is only embarked upon by the Anglican Church in very rare instances. Exorcists never work on their own but only with a team of reputable and experienced helpers, often with medical and psychiatric expertise as back-up. The book *Deliverance* does much to dispel the sensationalism which has grown up about the topic since the release of the film *The Exorcist* (1973) which was a highly fictionalised and exaggerated account of a poltergeist case at Mount Washington in the United States in 1949. A review of the story shows that parapsychologists and, indeed, the priests involved were largely sceptical of the paranormal aspects of the case.[40]

Of course, whether a Christian religious approach is appropriate will depend very much on the facts of the case and the beliefs of the individuals concerned; in Britain today there are many different faith communities as well as people of no belief.

If you arrive at the decision that the whole case is due to fraudulent behaviour or imagination, you can still send the papers to a leading society, stating of course your reasons for reaching your conclusion and marking your report "Confidential". Make it quite clear that names must not be published on any account.

Should you have completed the investigation to your satisfaction and have reached, in your opinion, a positive conclusion, act on the suggestion made earlier. Show the papers to a sceptical friend and ask for his/her comments. If he is convinced, then it is worth proceeding with forwarding the documents to a society or association.

---

[40] Horn, Stacy (2010) *Unbelievable Investigations into Ghosts, Poltergeists, Telepathy, and Other Unseen Phenomena, from the Duke Parapsychology Laboratory.* New York. Ecco Press.

One point that cannot be over-stressed is that it is essential to obtain permission to publish the material from the witnesses first. As you will find, many are still reluctant to have their names published, especially in connection with the controversial subject of ghosts. It is worth trying to persuade them to change their minds, however, for the strength and value of the report is affected if the names, addresses, and sometimes the occupations, of the people concerned cannot be given. To the suspicious, such omissions may cast doubt on the whole investigation. You can, of course, assure your informant that his/her name will, if it is so desired, be treated as confidential, and this should clearly be stated when forwarding on the material to the proper quarter.

Should you have formed a local research group, then obviously the report would be compiled with the agreement of and in consultation with your colleagues. Suitably edited it could well be considered saleable material to the general public; free copies could nevertheless be sent to relevant bodies.

It should be remembered that printing costs are high, and serious consideration should be given to publishing a number of reports, which will presumably be illustrated with photographs and sketches, both these are expensive items when it comes to reproduction.

One major outcome that usually results from a ghost-hunter's first serious investigation is a greater understanding of people's attitudes and the need for future enquiries. You may feel inclined to give up after completing one project, convinced that ghosts either do not exist, or even feeling that it does not matter anyway. Persevere until you have experience of several cases. Each one has its own peculiarities and interest. Even if you have to dismiss one case in the early stages because it is so obviously fraudulent, don't be discouraged – the next could be really fascinating and full of excitement.

Some cases will have to be frustratingly "shelved" due to desired information being unobtainable, certain individuals' refusal to be interviewed, or confirming records just not in existence. Remember, however, that some reports, provided the facts are accurate, are acceptable even though conclusions could not be reached. One of the major points that must be made clear and continually stressed to the witness is that "phantoms cannot hurt". Provide details of some of the other ghost stories of which you have knowledge in order to confirm this conclusion and build it up in a witness's mind. It is only when nervous characters are involved that any harm maybe caused, and that only mental. If the people affected show signs of psychological strain, then suggest that they have a chat with their doctor, but point out the logical argument that non-tangible phantoms are obviously incapable of carrying out any physical action.

It is for this reason, to quieten and reassure witnesses, that it may be necessary to impart some knowledge you have gained concerning the haunting.

Some individuals will rather sheepishly mention "the children". "We want to keep it from them and don't want to frighten them." If the ghost is of the average type (if there is such a thing) then the children will probably have experienced and accepted it anyway. Nervous parents are inclined to make nervous children. It is only when fright or agitation is outwardly shown by the adults that the child will need comfort. If the incidents are treated as "normal", and many people learn to accept them as such, then the tension will gradually disperse.

Many people have accepted the visitation of their ghost and have been mildly amused when friends and visitors expressed horror that the house was haunted. One lady in Chiddingford has "got so used to 'Charlie' now that we hardly notice when he has arrived." This is the perfect attitude, and should if possible be adopted by everyone who occupies a family property. The old adage familiarity breeds contempt could well be the philosophy to try and instil.

Having carried out your investigation you may find that other aspects of parapsychology have become more attractive and less expensive than ghost hunting. But there are not many spare-time occupations that will provide an insight into the unknown, and fewer still that have a chance of achieving the ghost hunter's aim of making the unknown known.

There is certainly a sense of achievement in having authenticated or disposed of a case of haunting, together with a feeling of satisfaction in assisting other people to understand and appreciate the serious aspects of ghost-hunting. It is also pleasant when one is able to calm and help someone suffering from his first ghost visitation.

But even if you are convinced that your first case was a waste of time or unproven, don't assume that *all* such cases are the same. *Not* all ghosts are fictional, they do exist, they are seen and heard, they have imparted knowledge (by telepathic processes) and will continue to do so until the human race becomes extinct.

And one must accept that *anyone* can see ghosts: members of the Royal family, Governmental ministers, dustmen. If you haven't yet seen an apparition there is always a chance, though as they only seem to appear when least expected don't try too hard.

It is hoped that this guide for potential ghost hunters has provided the reader with some fresh ideas for consideration, and that it may help to encourage more sophisticated investigation into the whole fascinating subject of parapsychology.

A FURTHER READING LIST

The following books and texts are recommended as reading for serious study of the paranormal and for learning about ghosts, poltergeists and hauntings. Some of them are classics in the field. They represent a wide range of views and opinions.

PSYCHICAL RESEARCH AND PARAPSYCHOLOGY

Anomalistic Psychology (2012) by Christine Simmonds-Moore, David Luke, and Chris French. UK. Palgrave Macmillan.

The Basic Experiments in Parapsychology (1984) by K. Ramakrishna Rao (Editor). USA. McFarland.

The Conscious Universe: The Scientific Truth of Psychic Phenomena (2009) by Dean Radin. USA. HarperOne.

Deviant Science: The Case of Parapsychology (1985) by James McClenon. USA. University of Pennsylvania Press.

Evidence for Psi: Thirteen Empirical Research Reports (2014) by Damien Broderick and Ben Goertzel (Editors). USA. McFarland.

Explaining the Unexplained: Mysteries of the Paranormal (1982) by Hans Eysenck, & Carl Sargent. UK. Weidenfield & Nicholson.

The Founders of Psychical Research (1968) by Alan Gauld. UK. Routledge & Kegan Paul.

An Introduction to Parapsychology (5th edition) (2007) by Harvey J. Irwin and Caroline Watt. USA. McFarland.

Investigating the Paranormal (2002) by Anthony Cornell. USA. Helix Press.

Natural and Supernatural: A History of the Paranormal from Earliest Times to 1914 (1977) by Brian Inglis. UK. Hodder & Stoughton.

Parapsychology: The Controversial Science (1991) by Richard Broughton. USA. Ballantine Books.

Parapsychology: Frontier Science of the Mind (1957, 2010) by J.B. Rhine and J.G. Pratt. USA. Kessinger Publications.

Psychical Research: A Guide to its History, Principles and Practices (1982) by Ivor Gratton Guinness. UK. Aquarian Press.

Parapsychology: Research on Exceptional Experiences (2005) by Jane Henry (Editor). UK. Routledge.

Psychical Research Today (1963) by Donald West. UK. Penguin Books.

Randi's Prize: What Sceptics Say About the Paranormal, Why They Are Wrong, and Why It Matters (2010) by Robert McLuhan. UK. Matador.

The Roots of Coincidence (1972) by Arthur Koestler. UK. Hutchinson.

Science and Parascience: A History of the Paranormal, 1914-1939 (1984) by Brian Inglis. UK. Hodder and Stoughton.

Science and Supernature: A Critical Appraisal of Parapsychology (1990) by James Alcock. USA. Prometheus Books.

The Society for Psychical Research: A History (1982) by Renee Haynes. UK. MacDonald.

Unbelievable: Investigations into Ghosts, Poltergeists, Telepathy and other Unseen Phenomena, from the Duke Parapsychology Laboratory (2010) by Stacy Horn. USA. Ecco Publications.

The Unexplained: Some Strange Cases of Psychical Research (1970) by Andrew MacKenzie. UK. Abelard-Schuman.

Varieties of Anomalous Experience (2000) by Ertzel Cardena, Steven J. Lynn and Stanley Krippner (editors) Washington, DC: American Psychological Association.

TELEPATHY, ESP AND PSYCHOKINSESIS

Anomalous Cognition: Remote Viewing Research and Theory (2014) by Edward C. May & S.B Marwaha (Editors). Jefferson, NC: McFarland.

A World in a Grain of Sand: The Clairvoyance of Stefan Ossowiecki (2005) by Mary Rose Barrington, Ian Stevenson, Zofie Weaver. USA. McFarland.

Dream Telepathy (3rd edition.) (2001) by Montague Ullman, Stanley Krippner, with Alan Vaughan. USA. Hampton Roads.

Entangled Minds: Extrasensory Experiences in a Quantum Reality (2006) by Dean Radin. New York. Simon & Schuster.

How to Test and Develop Your ESP (2001) by Paul Huson. USA. Madison Books.

The Imprisoned Splendour (1953) by Raynor C. Johnson. UK. Faber & Faber.

The Invisible Picture: A Study of Psychic Experiences (1981) by Louisa Rhine. USA. McFarland.

The Metal Benders: (1981) by John Hasted. UK. Routledge.

Mind-Matter Interaction: A Review of Historical Reports, Theory and Research (2011) by Pamela R. Heath. USA. McFarland.

The Nature of Mind: Parapsychology and the Role of Consciousness in the Physical World (1997) by Douglas M. Stokes. USA. McFarland.

The Physical Phenomena of Mysticism (1952) by Herbert Thurston. UK. Burns Oates.

Psychokinesis: A Study of Paranormal Forces through the Ages (1982) by John Randall. UK. Souvenir Press.

The Sense of Being Stared At and Other Unexplained Powers of Human Minds (2003) by Rupert Sheldrake. USA. Crown Publishers.

States of Mind: ESP and States of Consciousness (1975) by Adrian Parker. USA. Taplinger.

Telepathy: An Outline of Its Facts, Theory and Implications (1945) by Whatley Carington. UK. Methuen.

Twin Telepathy (1998, 2012) by Guy Lyon Playfair. White Crow Books.

SURVIVAL AND MEDIUMSHIP

Consciousness beyond Life: The Science of the Near Death Experience (2011) by Pim van Lommel. UK. HarperOne.

The Lazarus Effect (2013)by Sam Parnia. UK. Random House Group.

The Light Beyond (1988) by Raymond Moody and Paul Perry. USA. Macmillan.

The First Psychic: The Peculiar Mystery of a Notorious Victorian Wizard (2005) Paul Lamont. UK. Little Brown. (Study of the medium D.D Home)

Mediumship and Survival: A Century of Investigations (1983) by Alan Gauld. London: Paladin.

The Mediumship of the Tape Recorder (1978) by David Ellis. UK. D.J. Ellis Publishing.

Modern Spiritualism: A History and Spiritualism (2 vols) (1902) by Frank Podmore. UK. Methuen.

Human Personality and its Survival of Bodily Death (2 vols) (1903) by Frederic Myers. London: Longmans Green.

Immortal Remains:The Evidence of Life After Death (2003) by Stephen Braude. USA. Rowman & Littlefield Publishers.

Life Beyond Death: What Should We Expect? (2009) by David Fontana. UK. Watkins Publishing.

Mindsight (1999) by Kenneth Ring and Sharon Cooper. USA. William James Center for Consciousness Studies.

The Psychic Mafia (1976) by Lamar Keene. USA. St Martins Press.

Resurrecting Leonora Piper: How Science Discovered the Afterlife (2013) by Michael Tymn. UK. White Crow Books.

Sittings with Eusapia Palladino and other Studies (1963) by Everard Fielding. USA. University Books.

Religion, Spirituality and the Near-Death Experience (2003) by Mark Fox. UK. Routledge.

The Scole Report: An Account of an Investigation into the Genuineness of a Range of Physical Phenomena (2011) Montague Keen, Arthur Ellison and David Fontana (introduction by Alan Murdie). London. The Society for Psychical Research.

The Strange Case of Rudi Schneider (1985) by Anita Gregory. USA. The Scarecrow Press.

Science and the Afterlife Experience: Evidence for the Immortality of Consciousness (2012) by Chris Carter. USA. Inner Traditions.

The Survival of Man (1909) Oliver Lodge. UK. Methuen

The Varieties of Religious Experience (1902) William James. USA. Harvard University Press.

What Happens When We Die (2005) Sam Parnia. UK. Hay House.

OUT OF THE BODY EXPERIENCES

Beyond the Body (1982) by Susan J. Blackmore. UK. Heinemann

Otherworld Journeys: Accounts of Near Death Experiences in Medieval and Modern Times (1987) by Carol Zaleski. USA/UK. Oxford University Press.

Out-of-the-Body Experiences (1968) by Celia Green. UK. Hamish Hamilton.

APPARITIONS AND HAUNTINGS

Adventures in Time: Encounters with the Past (1997) by Andrew MacKenzie. UK. Athlone Press.

Apparitions (1975) by Celia Green, and Charles McCreery. UK. Hamish Hamilton.

Apparitions (1952) by G.N.M Tyrrell. UK. Duckworth.

Apparitions: An Archetypal Approach to Death, Dreams and Ghosts (1979) by Anita Jaffe. USA. Spring Books.

Apparitions and Haunted Houses (1939) by Ernest Bennett. UK. Faber & Faber.

Apparitions and Survival of Death (1973) by Raymond Bayless. USA. Carol Publishing.

Appearances of the Dead: A Cultural History of Ghosts (1982) by R.C. Finucane. USA. Prometheus Books.

The Borley Rectory Companion (2009) by Paul Adams, Eddie Brazil and Peter Underwood. UK. History Press.

A Brief Guide to Ghost Hunting: How to Investigate Paranormal Activity from Spirits and Hauntings to Poltergeists (2013) by Leo Ruickbie. UK. Robinson

Conversations with Ghosts (2014) by Alex Tannous with Callum E Cooper. UK. White Crow Books.

The Cheltenham Ghost (1948) by B. Abdy Collins. UK. Psychic Press.

The Departed Among the Living: An Investigative Study of Afterlife Encounters (2012) Erlendur Haraldsson.UK. White Crow Books.

The Encyclopaedia of Ghosts and Spirits (2007) by Rosemary E. Guiley. USA. Facts on File.

The Enigma of Borley Rectory (1996) by Ivan Banks (introduction by Andrew Green). UK. Foulsham.

Four Modern Ghosts (1958) by Eric Dingwall and Trevor Hall. UK. Duckworth.

A Gallery of Ghosts (1971) by Andrew MacKenzie. UK. Littlehampton Books.

Ghost Hunter's Guidebook (1986) by Peter Underwood. UK. Blandford Press.

The Ghost Hunter's Guidebook (1999) by Troy Taylor. USA. Whitechapel Productions.

Ghost Hunting: A Survivor's Guide (2012) by John Fraser. UK. History Press.

Ghosts Among Us (1994) by Harry Ludlam. UK. Janus Publishing Ltd.

Ghosts and Hauntings (1965) by Dennis Bardens. UK. Zeus Publishling

Ghosts Over Britain (1976) by Peter Moss. UK. David & Charles Publishers.

Ghosts of Today (1980) by Andrew Green. UK. David & Charles Publishers.

Ghost Writer (1966) by Fred Archer. UK. Psychic Press.

Ghostology (2016) by Steve Parsons. UK. White Crow Books.

Hauntings and Apparitions (1982) by Andrew MacKenzie. UK. Heinemann.

Hauntings and Poltergeists: Multidisciplinary Perspectives (2000, 2008) by James Houran & Rense Lange (editors) USA. McFarland.

Haunted Houses (1925) by Camille Flammarion. London. T.Fisher Unwin.

The Haunted (2007) by Owen Davies. UK. Palgrave.

The Haunted Inns of England (1972) by Jack Hallam. London. Wolfe Publications.

The Haunted Pub Guide (1984) by Guy Lyon Playfair. UK. Harrap & Co.

Haunted Houses You May Visit (1982) by Marc Alexander. UK. Sphere Books.

Haunted London (1973) by Peter Underwood. London. Harrap & Co.

The Haunting of Borley Rectory(1955) by Eric Dingwall, Kathleen Goldney and Trevor Hall. Duckworth.

The Hidden Powers of Nature (2002) by Manfred Cassirer. UK. D.J. Ellis Publications.

In Search of Ghosts (1995) by Ian Wilson. London. Headline.

New Light on Old Ghosts (1966) by Trevor Hall. London. Duckworth Ltd.

Our Haunted Kingdom (1973) by Andrew Green.UK. Wolfe Publishing.

Paranormal Acoustics (2015) by Steve Parsons & Cal Cooper. UK. White Crow Books.

Phantom Ladies (1976) by Andrew Green. London. David & Charles.

Science and the Spook (1971) by George Owen and Victor Simms. UK. Dobson.

Seeing Ghosts: Experiences of the Paranormal (2002) by Hilary Evans. UK. John Murray Publishing.

Some Unseen Power: Diary of A Ghost Hunter (1985) by Philip Paul.UK. Robert Hale Ltd.

Spectres of the Self (2010) by Shane McCorristine. UK. Cambridge University Press.

The Terror that Comes in the Night: An Experience-Centred Study of Supernatural Assault Traditions (1982) by David Hufford. USA. University of Pennsylvania Press.

True Ghost Stories of Our Time (1991) by Vivienne Rae-Ellis. UK. Faber & Faber.

Zones of Strangeness (2012) by Peter A. McCue. UK. AuthorHouseUK.

There are numerous popular regional and local books about ghosts and hauntings covering many cities and towns across the UK. Although these works often include much folklore they can assist in understanding the background to sites where paranormal activity is being reported today and give an insight on popular views which can shape perceptions. There are also a large number of books written by practising mediums and psychics providing personal accounts of experiences.

POLTERGEISTS

Can We Explain the Poltergeist? (1964) by A.R.G Owen. USA. Garrett/Helix.

Ghosts and Poltergeists (1953) Herbert Thurston. UK. Burns Oates.

Haunted People: The Story of the Poltergeist Down the Centuries. (1951) by Hereward Carrington and Nandor Fodor. USA. E.P. Dutton.

Poltergeists (1979) by Alan Gauld and Anthony Cornell. UK. Routledge & Kegan Paul.

This House Is Haunted. (1980, 2011) Guy Lyon Playfair. UK. White Crow Books.

On the Track of the Poltergeist (1986) D. Scott Rogo. USA. Prentice-Hall.

On the Trail of the Poltergeist (1958) Nandor Fodor. USA. Arco Publications.

The Poltergeist (1972) by William G. Roll. USA/UK. New American Library/ Star Books.

The Poltergeist Phenomenon (1996) by John and Anne Spencer. UK. Headline Books Ltd.

Poltergeists: A History of Violent Haunting (2011) by P.G. Maxwell-Stewart. UK. History Press.

The Poltergeist Experience (1979) by D. Scott Rogo. USA. Penguin.

South Shields Poltergeist: One Family's Fight Against An Invisible Intruder (2009) by Michael J. Hallowell and Darren Ritson. UK. History Press.

Unleashed: Poltergeists Murder and the Curious Story of Tina Resch (2004) by William Roll and Valerie Storey. USA. Pocket Books.

APPENDIX ONE – QUESTIONS FOR INVESTIGATORS

Once you have identified the name of the witness, their address and contact details, age and occupation and agreed any matters of confidentiality, it will be necessary to gather further information. Questions for witnesses and residents of allegedly haunted premises may include:

1. Where did your experience take place?

2.   When did the events begin?

3. What was the date of your experience?

4. What time was your experience?

5. When was the most recent experience or event?

6. How frequent are events at the moment compared with the past?

7. What other persons have had these experiences?

8. Who was the first to notice something strange was happening?

9. Were other witnesses aware of your experiences at the time?

10. Have there been experiences that were only experienced by some people and not others at the same time?

11. Have any pets or animals shown any unusual reactions?

12. Do apparitions resemble actual persons from the past? If so, give the reasons or evidence for thinking this.

13. Did the person who had the experience know about these persons beforehand?

14. Are any objects moved or disturbed? If so, which?

15. Has anyone seen an object start to move?

16. Do witnesses or anyone else have any ideas about the cause of the experiences or events?

APPENDIX TWO

TEMPERATURE MEASUREMENT WHEN GHOST HUNTING

Adapted and condensed from *Ghostology* (2015) by Steve Parsons.

(Reproduced with permission of the author. Copyright Steve Parsons (2015)

There is certainly a great deal of anecdotal evidence to link sudden or unexpected changes in ambient air temperature with reports of people experiencing unusual, possibly ostensibly paranormal events. Modern researchers using digital recording thermometers and thermal cameras have reported similar strange observations like those in the past. Currently there are no suitable explanations how and why these temperature anomalies can take place. Such anomalies are often coincident with a report of paranormal activity but apart from the coincidental nature of the measurement and the experience the two cannot as yet be directly linked.

Parapsychologists and sceptics often make a case for personal belief, suggestion or expectation being the link between a perceived temperature change and a paranormal event. Whilst this is true in many cases, perhaps the majority, it fails to take into account those rare instances where a proper objective measurement of temperature was made and it could be demonstrated that the temperature did indeed change in an unexpected manner or in a way that the recognised processes governing thermodynamics (the transfer of heat) currently does not explain.

Making measurements involves a series of steps that must be adhered to in order for any measurement to be considered meaningful. The correct instrument must be selected for the desired variable being measured. The proper unit must be selected and agreed for the variable being measured. The measuring instrument must be used correctly to ensure accuracy of the measurement. The calibration and precision of the measurement must be noted. It is important that the person making the measurements understands exactly what they are measuring and what instrument is required to make the correct measurements.

Types of thermometer

Liquid in glass (LIG) thermometers

These thermometers use the expansion of a liquid (mercury or alcohol) in response to an increase in temperature. The typical LIG thermometer consists of a sealed stem of uniform small-diameter tubing (capillary tube) made from glass or other transparent material with a larger diameter reservoir (bulb) at one end. Graduations on the stem form a temperature scale.

LIG thermometers are not reliable for surface temperature measurement being slow to respond to ambient temperature changes. LIG thermometers also rely upon a human operator and manual observation, generating the risk of reading errors.

Thermocouple (TC) thermometers

TC thermometers use the electromotive force, commonly referred to as 'emf' (not be confused with Electromagnetic Flux) which is the force or electrical potential (electrical voltage) that causes an electrical current to flow through a conductor. TC thermometers use two different metals, normally copper and constantan joined together, usually within a protective sheath or probe. A difference in the electric potential, which varies with temperature, exists at their junction. If a complete circuit forms with a second similar bi-metal junction at a different temperature, an electric current will flow and which can be measured using a galvanometer. This is known as the 'thermoelectric effect'. Most portable TC thermometers are used with battery powered circuits amplifying the very small voltage from the bi-metal junction, which drives a voltmeter that is directly calibrated with a temperature scale. Thermocouple thermometers are comparatively simple and robust, generally having fast response times (depending on the probe material). Modern microprocessor controlled TC thermometers can also be used to record temperature over time (data logging).

Resistance Thermometers (RTD)

These use the fact that most metals change their electrical resistance in response to changes in their temperature. Resistance thermometers typically respond readily and rapidly to ambient temperature changes, including to small fluctuations in temperature. Using meter or digital displays, the amount of resistance is measured and displayed using a scale calibrated in units of temperature. Microprocessor driven circuits can be used to record the temperature. The majority of modern consumer digital thermometers use one of the resistance techniques to measure temperature.

The types of thermometer described above (LIG, TC and RTD) all measure the temperature of the probe from physical changes within the probe material. By careful application of the probe the temperature of the medium it is attached to, or immersed within, can therefore be observed. Such devices are often known as direct reading or contact thermometers. It is important to note that the measured value they provide is only a measurement of the temperature of the sensor and the immediate area that surrounds it or with which it is in direct contact. It is therefore incorrect to assume a larger or surrounding area is at the same temperature. Using any single thermometer to measure the temperature of an entire room for instance will certainly give the user an erroneous result. In order to obtain an accurate assessment of the temperature of a room, it is required that a series of individual measurements are obtained throughout the space and the individual measurements considered either as a temperature gradient across the space or as a mean value for the entire space.

Infrared Thermometer (IRT)

IRTs do not measure temperature directly; instead they use the infrared (IR) emissions from the material to obtain its temperature. As such they are also known as non-contact thermometers. All objects emit IR in varying amounts depending on the material's emissivity and its temperature. The emissivity of a material (written 'e') is the relative ability of its surface to emit energy by radiation. In general, the duller and blacker a material may be, the closer its emissivity is to 1. The more reflective a material may be, then the lower its emissivity will be. IRTs are useful for measuring temperature under circumstances where TCs or other probe type sensors cannot be used or do not produce accurate data for a variety of reasons. Another further factor for consideration when using an IRT is the Distance to Spot (D:S) ratio; this is the ratio of the distance to the object and the diameter of the temperature measurement area. For instance if the D:S ratio is 12:1, measurement of an object 12 inches (30 cm) away will give an average of the temperature over a 1-inch-diameter (25 mm) area. As the D:S ratio increases the area being measured will increase but the overall accuracy of the temperature information may be reduced. Many IRT's also use a laser pointer to indicate the region being measured, usually taking the form of a simple red spot at the centre of the measuring region.

IRTs cannot be used for measuring air temperature. It is an all too common error made by ghost investigators who describe capturing and even measuring 'cold-spots' in the air within a location using IRTs. Air is thermally transparent with an emissivity value of Zero, neither absorbing or radiating any infrared energy and its temperature cannot be measured using this technology.

Thermal Imaging (TI)

Related to the IRT is the *Thermal Imaging (TI)* camera, which also utilises the principle of IR emission to infer the temperature of a material. Instead of simply displaying the result in terms of a temperature value, thermal imagers use the information from an array of individual IR sensors (pixels) built onto a silicon chip to form a visual representation of the temperatures present within the field of view of the camera. Thermal imaging cameras use a specialised focal plane array sensor (FPA) that responds only to longer IR wavelengths.

TIs are now being increasingly used by ghost hunters. Most models can be used with additional software to extract additional thermal information such as maximum, minimum and the spot temperature at any point within the picture. The resulting pictures (Thermographs) can allow quick visual comparisons between different parts of the image to be made.

Regarding the deployment of thermal cameras in ghost investigation there is really only anecdotal evidence to support their use value. Based upon the assumption that paranormal activity is linked to changes in temperature, either real or imagined, some investigators speculate that it might be possible to visualise a ghost or spirit using this technology. This assumption is unfounded there being simply no evidence that ghosts or spirits possess any thermal properties. Thermal cameras do not register changes in air temperature, for exactly the same reason as the IR thermometer; air does not give off or absorb infrared energy.

Whilst a number of standards exist for defining units of measurement such as the imperial system and the metric system, the majority of scientifically recognised measurement is now undertaken using the SI system of measurement; the abbreviation deriving from the French - *Système International d'Unités.* In addition, some variation of units exist within equipment manufactured mainly for local markets and specialist applications. For instance, many items of measuring equipment manufactured are intended for the USA market and display measurements using the US Customary Units system (derived from the British Imperial system), although most also offer SI measurements.

With thermometers, the Fahrenheit scale is still used in the United States rather than the (SI) Celsius scale, which is standard throughout the UK and Europe and other countries. It is therefore more important that the investigator chooses and uses one single system of measurement and units are not mixed.

Manufacturers of better quality instruments generally include an indication of a device's calibration; some may even provide or offer a calibration service and certificate of calibration. In terms of ghost investigating, all of the parameters that are routinely measured such as temperature and electromagnetic fields have defined standards for making measurements and documenting the results. Groups that adapt or build their own equipment in all likelihood lack any form of accurate calibration and the resulting data cannot be accurately related to any defined standard.

Recording Measurements

Once any measurement has been made it is vital the information is documented correctly and that those recording the information understand the recording methods being used. For investigators, this may take the form of a separate chart or information in personal notes. The units, either Fahrenheit or Celsius, must be agreed upon, as must the measuring method. Whatever method is adopted everyone participating in the investigation must employ it. With temperature anyone making the measurements must present their data in a form that can be related to everyone else making the same measurements. The data must be presented in a form that can be readily understood by the person transcribing that information, often at a later time or date. Without a standardised approach it is almost impossible to relate one set of measurements to another.

Failing to adequately document not only the measurements, but also the method and context in which they were obtained, will only result in any resulting conclusions that are drawn from that data being questionable and unreliable.

Measuring Temperature

As stated thermometers do not actually measure the temperature of the surface or material itself but instead measure either physical changes within the probe material or the thermal radiation emissions from an object. There are a number of ways that errors can be introduced into the measuring process and may seriously affect the overall accuracy of measurements.

Poor selection of equipment and poor positioning of the sensor can both lead to a misreading of the temperature. For example, an IRT or TI cannot be used to measure the air temperature. Locating a TC / RTD too close to a hot or cold object can result in the surrounding air temperature being affected by radiant heat from the surface. Probe type thermometers such as the TC and RTD are also only capable of taking the temperature from the material they are in direct or very close contact with and therefore cannot be used for temperature measurement over a large area. The actual region of temperature measurement is that which is directly in contact with the probe. Air has a poor capacity to conduct thermal energy and so in reality only a region of perhaps a few cubic inches around the probe may be accurately temperature sampled. Liquids tend to conduct thermal energy better and so permit a larger region around the probe to be sampled. Thus, simply taking one or two temperature readings within a room rarely results in an accurate temperature profile.

A better method might be to make a series of temperature measurements at regular (1 metre) intervals, both vertically (hot air rises, whilst cooler air falls) as well as horizontally. This will provide a range of ambient temperature observations for the entire room and an overall more accurate impression of the temperature within the space. This is obviously time consuming but in reality is the only way that it is currently possible to obtain accurate information. Using a TI can allow a rapid assessment of the surface temperatures to be made over a large area, as a series of thermographs can be taken for later examination in detail. However, the TI cannot be used for obtaining measurements of air temperature. The TI and IRT also rely for accuracy on the user correctly setting the emissivity calibration of the device.

Baseline Measurements

Baseline measurements are essential in many types of scientific measurement, to establishing a known value or reference point against which all subsequent measurements of the same variable can be compared. However, when it comes to ghost investigation, all too frequently, the baseline measurements are made hours before the actual required measurements are obtained and often under very different conditions. Measurements obtained in the middle of a cold dark night are set against a baseline taken during the daytime. Measurements in empty buildings are set against a baseline obtained when the same building is full of people. Sometimes baseline measurements from earlier site visits are employed, that may have been taken days or weeks in advance. Such baselines can provide no usable information and are more likely to simply mislead the user.

To be useful the baseline measurements need to be made under circumstances that are as close to the actual investigation measurements as is possible. Equipment that will turned off during the investigation should be turned off, people who will not be present should be absent and items such as windows, doors, heating and lighting set to the conditions that they will be in during the actual investigation measurement period. It is also wrong to assume that baseline measurements are carried out only prior to an investigation. Ideally, the baseline measurements should run continuously for a period beginning prior to the investigation and throughout the entire duration of the investigation period. Modern technology allows the recording of many physical properties such as temperature, humidity and electromagnetism to be recorded using data logging equipment so this need not be an onerous or time consuming task. Failing that, it is a simple method for members of the investigation team to manually record the information at regular fixed intervals. By making the baseline measurements meaningful it becomes much easier to then describe and relate any subsequent measurements that seemingly deviate unexpectedly from those reference points.

Emissivity is dependent on the type and nature of the materials being measured and can vary by a large amount even over a small distance. For example, a wall may be partially painted or may have a mirror or painting hung upon it. Fabrics, plastics and many building materials all have different emissivity values, altering the accuracy of any overall temperature measurements made using these techniques. Generally, an emissivity setting with an average value (typically 0.95) is used to deal with these situations and although absolute accuracy is sacrificed, the measurements will be useably accurate to within a few degrees.

By understanding the shortfalls of temperature measurement and the particular requirements of the chosen thermometer it is possible for the investigator to develop a range of techniques and tools in order to be able to obtain generally accurate temperature measurements. Simply wandering around a location taking one or two temperature measurements in a random fashion will just result in inaccurate and misleading temperature data being obtained.

Witnesses, even experienced investigators, can therefore be considered generally poor at judging temperature changes and even when temperature changes are experienced, they will frequently misreport or exaggerate their perception of the amount, or the rate of any temperature change. It is therefore unwise for any investigator to place great store on witness reports alone as a basis for documenting temperature changes during the investigation process.

Printed in August 2021
by Rotomail Italia S.p.A., Vignate (MI) - Italy